JILL AND THE RUNAWAY

Jill's summer holidays get off to a bad
start when she sprains her wrist on the
day before Chatton Show, but things
begin to look much brighter when
she becomes involved in organising a
gymkhana in aid of needy horses – and is
asked to show Mrs Darcy's Sandy Two
in the class for novice hacks. However,
trouble appears in the form of Dinah
Dean, who has a riding lesson which
she can't pay for, and generally makes
a nuisance of herself. Her escapades
reach their culmination on the day of the
gymkhana . . .

**More 'Jill' stories
available in Knight Books**

Jill and the Runaway

Ruby Ferguson

KNIGHT BOOKS
Hodder and Stoughton

Text copyright © 1954, 1993 Hodder and Stoughton Ltd

First published by Hodder and Stoughton Ltd 1954

This edition first published as Jill Enjoys Her Ponies in 1972 by Knight Books
Revised edition 1993

ISBN 0 340 59076 9

Printed and bound in Great Britain for Hodder and Stoughton Books, a division of Hodder and Stoughton Ltd, Mill Road, Dunton Green, Sevenoaks, Kent TN13 2YA (Editorial Office: 47 Bedford Square, London WC1B 3DP) by Cox & Wyman Ltd, Reading, Berks. Typeset by Hewer Text Composition Services, Edinburgh.

Contents

1 A disappointed jumper

I was sitting on a pile of gravel outside a field gate feeling absolutely browned off. I don't mean a bit fed up, I mean practically crying like a small kid. I wouldn't have wished my worst enemy to feel so awful, not even Susan Pyke or my cousin Cecilia, and they are the worst blots I know.

It was the day of Chatton Show, the biggest event of the riding year in our part of the world, and every single person I knew would be there – except Me.

I had got a strained wrist. Not anything really bad like a fracture or even a sprain, but just a stupid strained muscle; and I hadn't even got it out riding, I had got it by swinging the bucket too far when I came back from feeding Mummy's unspeakable hens.

I always swing an empty bucket, and I dare say you do too, and all I can say is – don't, if you want to have any chance of riding your pony for days after.

The only thing I had thought of and talked about for a long time before this vile and shattering accident was Chatton Show. (That is to say, I had thought in slight spasms about the end-of-term exams, though not very much, according to my headmistress, who wrote unsympathetically on my report, 'Jill can do anything she gives her mind to and would be advised to give it more consistently to Mathematics, History, and

French.' What I admire about Miss Grange-Dudley is the marvellous way she expresses herself, like Shakespeare.)

It was my last chance to win the fourteen-and-under jumping, so of course I intended to do it. Next year I would be fifteen and competing with a crowd of very hard sixteen-year-olds who had gained all their experience in bigger shows than Chatton.

When I swung the bucket and my arm hurt, I just said Ouch! and took no more notice, but you can imagine my feelings when I woke up on the morning before the show with an arm like a Swiss roll.

I rushed into Mummy's room with a face lined and drawn with horror, as it says in thrillers, and cried, 'Mummy! Do something about my arm. Get it down or scrape it or something!'

She looked at it and said, 'Oh, dear. I'm afraid it's not much good, Jill. You should have gone to the doctor last night, as I seem to remember suggesting.'

'It wasn't bad last night,' I mumbled. 'It hardly hurt at all.'

I didn't want to admit that Mummy had known best, as she usually did.

'I'll go to the doctor now,' I said hopefully.

'Yes, do,' she said, not so hopefully.

So I went. I wore my jodhpurs and my fawn coat and my new red and fawn checked tie to show that I was a serious-minded person, and I sat in Dr Fisher's waiting-room for half an hour with two old women who were doing a sniffing duet, and a dim sort of boy with a dirty bandage on his leg, and some other faded-looking characters.

At last it was my turn. When I got home, Mummy said, 'Cheer up, Jill. I was afraid it wasn't going to be good news.'

'It isn't going to be any use for four days,' I said, and added, 'I don't want to go on living.' I then rushed upstairs and lay across my bed and wondered if anybody in the world had ever been so miserable before.

Mummy shouted upstairs, 'Are you coming down, Jill? Ann and Diana are here.' (My two riding friends.)

I yelled, 'Tell them to go away.'

But they didn't go away. They came up and said all the usual things. The more people tell you how sorry they are for you the worse you feel and the more you want to slay them.

'How dreary having to stand by the rails and watch us ride,' said Diana.

'I shan't,' I said. 'I'm not going.'

'Not going!' said Ann. 'You don't mean you're not going to Chatton Show?'

'I'd die,' I said.

'Well, you know best,' said Diana, 'but if it was me wild horses wouldn't keep me away. I mean, missing Chatton Show!'

I told her she needn't keep saying it.

'If you don't go, you'll wish you'd gone,' said Ann.

'I shan't,' I said.

'But what on earth will you do?' said Diana. 'I mean, there isn't anything on earth to do tomorrow but go to Chatton Show.'

'I'll read a good book,' I said bitterly. 'And I wish you'd both go away. I hate you.'

'Oh, we are sorry for you,' said Ann. 'We think it's the most awful bad luck that ever happened to anybody in the world.'

'And it's your last chance in the under-fourteens,' said Diana.

'Really?' I said sarcastically. 'I hadn't thought of that.' (Actually I hadn't thought of anything else.)

When I told Mummy I wasn't going to the show she said, 'I think you're being awfully silly.'

'I couldn't bear it,' I said in a sort of night-must-fall voice.

'But wouldn't you like to go with Mrs Lowe and Martin and me in the car and watch, and have a chicken lunch and ices, and see the Open Jumping?'

'No,' I croaked.

'Oh, Jill, you are a fool.'

'OK,' I said.

'But what will you do? You can't just hang about the cottage alone. Everybody will be at the show. You'll be bored stiff.'

I gave an awful gulp, like an expiring cow, and dashed upstairs again to bury my head in the pillow.

Of course the day of the show had to be the most gorgeous summer's day you ever saw. I tried not to notice the blue, blue sky and the bits of cottonwool cloud, and the sunshine spilling gold on the fields and the warm smell of grass and flowers. I wasn't quite such a beast as to wish it was raining to spoil the show for everybody else, but I did think Nature needn't have been quite so mean to me.

I got up and put on my gingham school dress and some pretty-far-gone gym shoes, and tried not to

think of my beloved riding clothes hanging spruce
and brushed in the cupboard.

At a quarter past ten the Lowes drove up in their
car to call for Mummy. There were Mr and Mrs
Lowe and Martin, all in light summer clothes.
I tried to look cool and don't-carish. I thought,
if they tell me to Look on the Bright Side and
Some-girls-haven't-got-any-arms-at-all I'd burst into
flames, but they didn't.

Mrs Lowe said, 'Not going, Jill?' and Martin said,
'Well, nobody's going to make you.'

Mummy got into the car in her cool cream silk
jacket and skirt and pretty straw hat, and said, 'Now
do eat a proper lunch, Jill, it's all in the fridge,
not just toast and jam,' and I said, 'All right,'
and looked heroic and waved them off with my
good hand.

And the minute they were gone, believe it or
believe it not, I wished with all my heart I had gone
too and hadn't been such a fool.

I thought of a few other things as I walked slowly
down to the orchard to my puzzled-looking ponies,
who, of course, were wondering why they weren't
going to the show for which they had been practising
for weeks. Black Boy and Rapide lifted their heads
from cropping the sweet orchard grass and fixed four
lovely dark eyes on me. I was remembering how
when I was a raw kid of ten and had just bought
my first pony, and couldn't afford riding lessons
and didn't even know how I was going to stable
and feed Black Boy in the winter, Martin Lowe had
made himself my friend and taught me to ride and
helped me to solve all my problems. And he did it

from a wheel-chair too, because he was paralysed and couldn't walk.

Mr and Mrs Lowe had been marvellous to me too, and invited me to their beautiful horsy home where there were lovely papers lying abut, like *Horse and Hound* and *Riding*, not the dreary magazines you find in most people's houses, all about knitting and love and how to make puddings.

So by now I was feeling the pangs of remorse, and I didn't even want the block of milk chocolate which Mummy had left on the kitchen table for a surprise for me.

The ponies looked a bit ragged, but I didn't see how I could groom them with only one hand. I fetched them some water, after sloshing a lot of it over my feet, and listened to them happily blowing into the bucket.

Black Boy was a bit small for me now but I could still make him do anything I wanted. I knew he would have won the under-fourteen jumping for me, and I had entered Rapide as my second horse, because on his day he could be brilliant. They were both trained to the last inch. But it wasn't much good thinking about things like that.

I waggled my wrist. It felt a bit better. I thought, *it would*! And I'll be jumping again in a week when it doesn't matter.

The morning seemed endless. I tried to read a thriller, but could only think what a din our help, Mrs Crosby, was making with the Hoover. Every time she passed the sitting-room door she shoved her head in and said, 'Having a nice read, dear? Why not go out and get a bit of fresh air? It don't do to brood.'

I said sarkily, 'Are you addressing a hen?' and she said, 'You don't know what real trouble is, you don't,' and I said, 'Oh, dry up!' – for which Mummy would have given me a good telling off if she had heard me.

That infuriated Mrs C. who said, 'And you've left your room in a shocking mess, I must say,' and I said, 'Well, what can I do with only one arm?' and that was asking for it, because she began to tell me about the daughter of the woman that her sister worked for who had both arms in splints for months and taught herself to paint pictures with her toes – 'lovely lifelike apples, ever so rosy' – and in the middle I got up and walked out, and Mrs Crosby said, 'If there's one thing I can't stick it's a great baby!'

In spite of what Mummy had said I didn't want any lunch. I took a pear and some biscuits and walked along the lane until I got to the heap of gravel which the road-menders had dumped outside a field gate. I sat down on it and thought, Help! There's hours and hours to wait yet.

And this is where you came in.

2   Other people's luck

After what seemed a lifetime I thought I had better go home, because apart from anything else there were the ponies and hens to feed. You might think that in the country it would be possible to get somebody to come and help with one's hens, but such is not the case. Most farm workers, having millions of hens to look after as part of their daily toil, take a dim view of going out of their way to feed and clean anybody else's mere eight.

It is surprising what you can do with one hand if you have time, and when I had done the feeding, and spilt more than the unfortunate creatures got, I went into the cottage and had some tea and toast, and waited for the car to come back, and every minute seemed an hour like it does in novels.

The sun still poured down and it had been the most perfect afternoon, and I had pictured it all in my mind, the spacious ring and the white-painted jumps, the stands crowded with spectators, the collecting ring and my friends waiting on their ponies under the trees feeling like one does while waiting for one's number to be called, and horses everywhere, flying tautly over the bars or swishing their tails in the paddock, or having coloured rosettes pinned to their cheekbands by lucky winners.

It was past seven o'clock when I heard sounds outside, ponies' hoofs, not the car with my returning mother. It was my friends, Ann and Diana, who knew I would be longing for news and had come straight from the show to tell me about it.

They both looked hot and dusty and happy.

'Are you still alive?' cried Ann as they came up the path. 'Everybody was saying, why hadn't you come.'

'Was it good?' I managed to say.

'Oh, the best ever. Don't think I'm being beastly, but it was. It was marvellous.'

'Who won the under-fourteen jumping?' I managed to gasp.

Diana pulled the knot of her yellow tie from under her ear, and said, 'A boy called Marshall that nobody had ever heard of. They're new people who've taken Mile End Farm. He was pretty hot, nobody else stood an earthly. He did three clear rounds, the competition round and two jumps-off. It literally paralysed you to see him. You know, one of these wonder-jumpers! Then he entered for the under-sixteens and was first in that too.'

'He wasn't! Not first in both classes?'

'Yes he was. He was great!'

'Then I don't suppose I'd have had a chance, even if I'd ridden?' I said.

'Well, even if you'd done a clear round in the competition you'd have had to have jumped it off, and jumped it off with this Marshall boy for ever and ever.'

'How old is he?'

'Just thirteen,' said Ann. 'He's got another year

in the under-fourteens, so what a hope for anybody else.'

'And if he's already won the under-sixteens too,'
I said, 'what a hope for us next year! Go on, tell me
some more. What did everybody I know do?'

'Wendy Mead was second in the Class C jumping
on Mrs Darcy's Cocktail.'

'Oh, jolly good!' I said, feeling a bit more like
myself.

'And I was third in the Child's Pony Self-Groomed
and Schooled,' said Diana modestly.

'Nice work!' I said. 'Who was second in the
under-fourteen jumping, anyway?'

There was a slight pause.

'Me,' said Ann, going red under her dust.

'You dope!' I shouted, frightfully pleased. 'Why
didn't you say so before? Where's your rosette?'

'I took it off George,' said Ann, opening her pocket
enough for me to see the blue ribbon. 'I didn't want
to look showing-off when you were having such a
terrible disappointment.'

'I feel all right now,' I said. 'I was a fool not to
go. I wish I'd gone.'

'How's the wrist?' said Diana.

'Better,' I said. 'Too late to be any good, of
course.'

'Well, there's Moorside next Saturday.'

'Moorside!' I said scornfully. 'All kids from riding
schools.'

'Well, who isn't a kid from a riding school?' said
Diana. 'I like that, coming from you! Who do you
think you are?'

'You wouldn't have a cold drink handy?' asked

Ann in a dusty sort of voice, and I took them in the kitchen and they drank four glasses of water each, and there was only enough orange squash in the bottle to go into two of them, and even then it was weak.

Suddenly the Lowes' car drew up, and we all rushed to the garden gate.

'Congratulations, Ann,' said Mrs Lowe. 'You rode beautifully and you should have won. That Marshall boy was hardly human. You would hardly expect to be up against competition like that in the under-fourteens.'

'Ann was awfully good, Jill,' said Mummy, looking at me to see how I was taking all this, and I said, 'I'm jolly glad,' and everybody looked relieved.

'I've never seen better open jumping,' said Mr Lowe, 'and I've been going to Chatton Show ever since I can remember. Harvey Smith won it, he was superb. And we all saw Summertime.'

'Oooh!' breathed Diana. 'I wish I was a famous rider and could go all over the country with a famous horse, jumping in open competitions.'

'You may be some day,' said Martin Lowe.

'But Daddy would never let me go and work in a famous stable,' said Diana. 'I've got to be a dreary physiotherapist.'

'But you've still got two more years in the juvenile classes,' said Ann, 'and so have I and so has Jill, and one never knows, the Marshall boy's farmer parents might be ruined and have to leave the farm before next Chatton Show.'

'If you were my daughter,' said Mummy severely, 'I should feel compelled to point out to you that opposition is a challenge, not something to wish removed by the hand of Fate.'

'Gosh, Mrs Crewe!' said Diana. 'Anybody can tell you are an author. You talk just like a frightfully learned book.'

Mrs Lowe took me on one side and said, 'Would you like to do something interesting these holidays, Jill?'

I nearly said yes, but not quite. I said Um, because you know how it is with grown-ups, their ideas of what is interesting are often quite different from yours. I mean, Mrs Lowe is a very good sort, but I certainly didn't want to learn hand-weaving or go to French classes or take somebody's baby out.

'Would it be anything to do with horses?' I said doubtfully.

She laughed and said, 'I wouldn't dare suggest anything to you that wasn't to do with horses. I know you too well. You'll probably be hearing from a friend of mine in a few days. She asked me to suggest some people's names to her, and I gave her yours.'

She wouldn't tell me any more, but I thought as long as the interest was horsy it couldn't be too bad. Anyway, it couldn't be sewing or prams.

In a few days my wrist was all right, and I was riding again. Then the postman brought a letter for me. I am always so excited when I get a letter that I can never open it properly, but tear the envelope across, which infuriates Mummy who uses a paper knife even if she has to go and find it first. This is known as Patience, which is a virtue I haven't got.

I looked at the beginning of the letter, which said

'Dear Jill,' and then at the end which said, 'Yours sincerely, Phyllis Whirtley.'

I said, 'It's from somebody I never heard of. Perhaps it's an aged crone that I once helped across the road, and she's left me a Highland castle or something in her will.'

'Oh, I do hope it's a Highland castle!' said Mummy. 'Jill, that's no way to treat a letter. Flatten it out and read it properly.'

I propped the letter against the coffee pot (we were in the middle of breakfast) and the coffee pot fell over. You wouldn't think a light little thing like a letter could knock over a coffee pot, but then you don't know the kind of things that happen to me unless you have read my previous books. The funny thing was, there was about ten times as much coffee all over the table as there had been in the pot. I sat thinking how this could be, while Mummy mopped frantically and tried to save the butter and marmalade from the flood, and then she said, 'Do read it! What does it say?'

'It's from somebody called Phyllis Whirtley,' I explained. 'I think she must be that friend of Mrs Lowe's. She says, "Blossom Hall, August, Dear Jill" – what a nerve!'

'What a what?' said Mummy, in surprise.

'Oh, that isn't in the letter, only I do think people are the utter depths to call you Jill when they don't know you, as if you were about six.'

Mummy said she had had her doubts about that Highland castle, and could I possibly bear to read the letter without any more interruptions.

It said, 'Dear Jill, I am trying to collect a group of

young people who are keen on horses to help me in an interesting project I have in mind.'

I stopped at this point, and said, 'Gosh! She sounds like our English teacher.'

'Go *on*!' said Mummy.

I read out, 'I should be so pleased if you would come and meet the others at my house on Friday afternoon of next week, and stay for tea. Come on your pony if you like, but do try and come. We have a mutual friend in Mrs Lowe who says you are just the kind of person I want.' 'Sounds a bit sinister, don't you think?'

Mummy asked, what was the interesting project? and I said, 'She doesn't say. She is probably afraid of putting me off. She says, "If you have a friend of like mind with yourself, do bring her along." What on earth does "like mind" mean?' I began to giggle.

Mummy said that either Ann or Diana would do.

'It will have to be Ann,' I said, 'because Diana will be in London next week. I suppose I'll have to go. But what on earth do you think it's all about?'

The summer holidays only come once a year after all, and you spend the greater part of the year looking forward to them, and then they seem very short. In our part of the world there are pony shows each Saturday in August, and one trains hard for these all through the early part of the summer. After all, they are the real test of what you and your ponies can do, and you compete with other people of your own age who have also been schooling hard all the year round.

I wasn't at all keen on the idea of anything interfering with my August programme. It's a funny thing, but grown-ups always seem to think you're short of something to do in the summer holidays. I hate being organised, because I am perfectly capable of planning every single thing I am going to do in the summer holidays, and so I could if they were twice as long, and so can any other person who has a stable with two perfectly good ponies in it.

My friend Ann Derry wouldn't welcome outside interference either. Though unfortunate enough to have the kind of mother who employs a groom and cannot bear to see her darling daughter with a dandy brush in her hand, from the first Ann firmly insisted on doing her pony, George, herself and he was one of the loveliest ponies I have ever seen. I felt she hadn't quite the knack of showing him to the best advantage – showing was not her strong point – but George was particularly good at jumping and gymkhana events and had a full August programme in front of him.

So you can see why I wasn't wild with excitement at getting mixed up with this Mrs Whirtley. However, I was willing to view the prospect with an open mind. Anyway, I didn't let it worry me.

3 My frightful pupil

Black Boy and Rapide were badly in need of some jumping practice. Their week of idleness hadn't done them any good. They had put on weight and become lazy, so I took them up to the riding school where they proceeded to play me up in fine style.

Neither of them wanted to jump, and each in turn refused at the first fence. Then they went on to amuse themselves by pretending they didn't know what the jumps were for. Black Boy, who was always a bit of an actor, would sidle along in a very stagy way, tossing his head and swinging his rump, and suddenly arriving at the jump would look at it in pained surprise, widening and rolling his eyes affectedly, while Rapide, tied to the fence, stood looking on and making faces. When his turn came he copied Black Boy – as he always did for better or worse – and gave an even more ham performance.

I made them both go right round the seven jumps, while top bars went clattering down, and after Black Boy had eaten half the three-foot hedge while I was tightening Rapide's cheek strap which he had loosened by throwing his head about, I tied them both and walked back across the paddock red with shame and fury.

'I'd disqualify you at sight,' said Wendy Mead,

shaking with laughter. She was the girl who helped Mrs Darcy with the riding school, and her father's farm was nearly next door.

'I'd disqualify myself,' I said in disgust. 'What an exhibition, and I thought my ponies were foolproof! This is what comes of a week's rest out at grass.'

'I've come to the conclusion that any pony is capable of anything,' said Wendy. 'They've played you up thoroughly this morning, but you'll soon get them in hand again. By the way, Jill, if you've got half an hour to spare I wish you'd do me a favour.'

I told her I was boiling hot so I hoped it was something cool that she wanted me to do, and that I had to be home by twelve.

'Well, would you take a lesson for me?' she said. 'I don't know what I was thinking about, but I've booked two lessons for the same time.'

'Honestly,' I said, 'at the present moment I don't feel capable of teaching a four-year-old to sit on a seaside donkey.'

'Well, this is quite unimportant. A beginner. She rang up and booked a course of six lessons, and this will be the first.'

'Oh, all right,' I said without much enthusiasm. 'Only you know what beginners are. They bounce up on an unschooled pony, and want to gallop and jump before they can walk properly.'

'This one isn't bringing a pony, so you can put her on anything you like.'

'Well, can I have a look at Blue Smoke first?' I asked.

We went round to the stable, and in her stall stood Mrs Darcy's beautiful grey hunter, shining like satin, and turning her lovely head for our caresses. I made a lot of flattering remarks about her beauty, and thought that if I could ever own anything like her my life's ambition would be achieved.

'Do you remember that awful time when James Bush rode her, and she was ill afterwards, and we thought she was dying?' I said.

Wendy was just opening her mouth to reply when I thought I heard a sound like a shuffle of feet.

'What's that?' I said, and as we both listened we saw a small dark shadow move somewhere at the end of the line of stalls.

'There's somebody there,' said Wendy, 'who has no business to be there.' She called sharply, 'Come out, you – whoever you are!'

The weirdest little person appeared, and came sidling towards us, looking scared stiff. She looked about eight, and she had on a school skirt and washed-out tee-shirt, with black tights, and her hair hung over her eyes which peeped out from under her fringe like two black buttons in a bird's nest.

'Who on earth are you?' said Wendy.

The kid looked terrified, and said she was sorry but she just wanted to look at the horses.

'Well, you shouldn't be in here, you know,' said Wendy. 'Now run along home, quick!'

'But I've come for my l-lesson,' said the kid.

Wendy gave a groan, rolled up her eyes, and extended one hand dramatically towards me.

'Methinks 'tis your pupil,' she said. 'Take it, Jill, it's all yours.'

'Murder!' I said, under my breath. But Mrs Darcy had always insisted on extreme politeness to clients however off-putting they might look, and as one who has had a lot of experience of riding schools I can tell you that new pupils often look very off-putting indeed. (As a matter of fact, I did myself when I was a new pupil.) So I pulled myself together and said to the kid, 'Good morning. Will you come outside and tell me what you want? What's your name, by the way?'

'Dinah Dean,' said the kid, who looked even smaller and thinner when we got out into the daylight.

I asked her how old she was, and she said she was nearly thirteen. I looked surprised and said, 'Have you done much riding?'

She looked a bit miserable and said, 'I – I'm afraid I haven't ever been on a pony. I expect you won't want me here, not knowing anything about riding.'

'Oh, we'd much rather,' I said. 'We hate beginners who think they know everything before they start. Give me raw material every time.'

I got that last remark out of a book called *Raoul the Riding Master* and it came in handy and the kid looked very impressed.

'What shall I put her on?' I asked Wendy, and Wendy said, 'Oh, Ninepins, I should think.' Ninepins was the riding school's nice old slug, fifteen years old and very understanding with beginners.

'Come on then,' I said to the kid. 'First we go to the harness room and fetch the tack. Would you know anything about a pony's tack?'

'I suppose it would have a bridle and a s-s-saddle,' she stuttered.

'Look, would you mind not being so shy?' I said.

'You're quite right. I've known beginners who didn't even know what tack was.'

I collected Ninepins' tack, and then went along, followed by the kid, to get the pony.

'Oh, isn't he sweet!' she said, throwing her arms round his neck. I felt a bit more taken with her, because she obviously loved ponies, and Ninepins who hadn't been called sweet for years looked very bucked up.

'I suppose you haven't the slightest idea how to put the bridle on?' I asked.

'I wouldn't know anything,' she said, with a shy grin that got lost in her floppy hair.

'Well, let's get cracking,' I said. 'First we slip the reins over his head and neck, and next we stand close to his head and pass the right arm round and under, taking hold of the crown piece with the right hand and the bit with the left.' I went on with the usual instructions, and finished up, 'It sounds complicated when you say it, but it's awfully easy really, when you get the knack.'

She looked a bit doubtful and said, 'How does the saddle go on?'

I showed her how to run the stirrups up the leathers, and how to fling on the saddle and fasten the girths properly, and she watched so closely that I could feel her breathing down my arm. I slid my fingers down the girths to smooth out wrinkles, and she said, 'I think that's a good idea. I'd like to learn to put the tack on properly' – which was better than most beginners who think that saddling a pony is just like tying up a brown paper parcel.

'Have you any idea how to mount?' I said.

'I don't know anything,' she said, 'I expect you think I'm awful.'

'Don't be silly,' I said. 'I'll put you up the first time, and then I'll teach you to mount properly by yourself.'

To my surprise she went up quite lightly, and did all I told her, and sat straight with her knees and head up and her hands well down. Apart from looking so awful she didn't look bad at all – if you know what I mean.

'Ooh, this is gorgeous!' she said. I suddenly realised that the kid was having a sort of dream-come-true feeling, and I felt a bit sympathetic. Actually the first time I got on a pony I was far worse than Dinah Dean.

I started Ninepins off at a slow walk, and Dinah looked thrilled. She seemed to have those naturally light hands that people are born with, and she must have watched people riding because I could tell she was copying what she had seen and was trying to do it right.

I said, 'What school do you go to? I think I've seen you somewhere before.'

She turned red and said, 'I don't go to school. I sort of keep house and cook and all that for Daddy.'

I said that I thought people had to go to school, and she said, 'You see, we're always moving, and nobody notices me. Can I get off now, and learn to mount by myself?'

I was quite surprised and impressed, because the last thing most beginners want to do is to get down and learn to mount properly. They usually want to gallop and try a few jumps.

I showed her how to mount, and she soon got the idea. She really was the best beginner I'd ever had anything to do with, if she hadn't looked so awful and made me cold inside in case anybody I knew would come along the lane and watch us and think what a terrible advertisement she was for the riding school. Then I suddenly remembered where I had seen her before. She had once come up and patted Black Boy when I had tied him outside the Post Office, and I had shooed her off.

If she recognised me she hadn't shown it. I let her do a complete round of the paddock by herself and she did quite well and looked to be in a sort of daze of joy, and then I thought, Thank goodness the half-hour's up!

I brought her in and said, 'Well, that's all for now. I suppose you've arranged with Miss Mead for your next lesson?'

Dinah went bright scarlet, and I thought she was going to cry.

She blurted out, 'I'm not coming any more.'

'Well, that's up to you,' I said, surprised. 'But you're not bad at all, and you'd be quite good after a few more lessons.'

'It was a lovely lesson,' she said, 'but – well, I can't pay for it. I thought I'd have the lessons and then find some way of paying for them, but I can't. I expect you'll feel like sending me to prison.'

I thought, that's the limit. People who run a riding school or any sort of business, do occasionally come across characters who think it is clever to do cheating things like that. I remembered how when I was helping some friends of mine to run a stable and hire out hacks, there was a woman who got a pony for a whole week for her child for nothing, by giving us a false name and address. I suppose she thought because we were only young she had twisted us very cleverly, and we were sorry for her child for having a mother like that.

Up to then I had been feeling a bit sorry for the Dean kid, but now I was just plain furious. I didn't know how I was going to tell Wendy Mead, and I hoped she wouldn't think I was in any way to blame.

I said very coldly, 'You shouldn't have come. We don't teach people to ride for the fun of it. Now get out of here and don't ever come back again.'

I led Ninepins away and never looked back to see what Dinah was doing. I said to Wendy, 'That was a wash-out. The kid had a lesson and then calmly said she couldn't pay for it.'

'The little beast!' said Wendy. 'We've had that kind before. And she'd the nerve to book six lessons! Well, I'll be on the look-out for her if she ever turns up here again. Thanks, Jill, I'm sorry your time has been wasted.'

I collected my ponies, and Wendy said, 'Don't worry about them misbehaving. They know perfectly well what they're supposed to do. When are you using them again?'

'Saturday,' I said, 'at Moorside. It's rather a kiddish affair but it's all practice.'

'It was rotten luck missing Chatton Show.'

'You're telling me!' I said. 'By the way, congrats on winning the Grade C jumping.'

'Oh that was just a fluke,' said Wendy modestly.

Black Boy and Rapide looked as meek and innocent as if they had done a perfect morning's work.

'Oh, come on, you two perishers!' I said.

4　This pride and fall business

I was late home, which annoyed Mummy as she had planned an early lunch so that she could catch a bus to Rychester, and I had to explain. When I told her about Dinah she said, 'That must be the child I was hearing about. Everybody seems sorry for her. Her father does some kind of research and keeps this child cleaning the house and cooking. He could be made to send her to school, but I believe they never stay anywhere long and she wouldn't be much better off. They live in one of those hard-looking little houses on the new estate.'

'She had a perfectly good riding lesson for nothing,' I said, 'and wasted half my morning.'

Mummy looked thoughtful and said, 'I don't like to think that a child wants a lesson so badly that she'll cheat to get one.'

'Oh, some kids would try anything on,' I said, feeling at the same time a sneaking feeling that Dinah wasn't really that type of kid. I added, 'I never had anything I didn't pay for.' But the minute I'd said it I remembered that I had had practically everything without paying for it, just because Martin Lowe had given me my first lessons and my feeding stuff and a lot of other things.

I said, 'Well, anyway, I did jobs to pay for Black

Boy's winter keep, and I bought my first riding coat and jodhpurs secondhand at an auction.'

'And it was my money, if I remember rightly,' said Mummy musingly, and added, 'How much would a lesson cost like the one you gave Dinah Dean?'

'Ten pounds,' I said.

She took some money out of her purse and said, 'Give that to Mrs Darcy. Then the riding school won't be the loser.'

'You needn't – ' I began, but she already had on her faraway look which means she is thinking about some of those very whimsy characters she puts into her children's books. I sometimes think it's a good thing that the children in Mummy's books don't go to my school or they'd be murdered. She had just had her latest one published, called *Angeline, the Fairy Child*, about a person who was only six and brought joy and gladness into the heart of her bitter old grandfather, and there had been eleven frightfully good reviews of it in eleven frightfully good papers, and Mummy was thrilled, but it just left me cold.

I went around to see Ann that night and found her fussing and fuming over a slight cut on George's knee that you could hardly see.

'Our kid Pam did it,' she said. 'She'd no business to ride George, I've told her a million times she's not to touch him. Now he'll lose joint-oil. He'll be scarred for life.'

I told her it was nothing and you could hardly see it.

'He'll be stiff on Saturday for Moorside gymkhana,' fumed Ann.

'He won't,' I said. 'Gosh, you are a fusspot,

Ann. Put some penicillin powder on it. It's only a scratch.'

'I bet it turns septic,' she grumbled.

'If it does I'll lend you Black Boy for Saturday,' I said. 'Anyway, Moorside is nothing. You know we only enter for it because Mrs Darcy says it looks unsportsmanlike to shun the smaller gymkhanas just because we're good.' Then to cheer her up I told her about Mrs Whirtley and the Interesting Project, and asked her if she'd like to go with me as my other horsy person.

'But what's it all in aid of?' said Ann suspiciously, just as I knew she would.

I told her I hadn't a clue, she knew just as much about it as I did.

I added, 'The Whirtley woman is a friend of Mrs Lowe's, and Mrs Lowe is so decent and knows how I feel about the things I do in the summer holidays that I don't think she'd deliberately get me mixed up in anything I didn't care about.'

'The summer holidays are so jolly short,' said Ann. 'I mean, we don't want to do anything but ride, do we? I mean, supposing it's getting up a Bring and Buy Sale! We tried that once and we weren't so hot at it. Even Mrs Lowe likes Bring and Buy Sales, and so does my mother and yours too, if it comes to that. I can't think of anything drearier.'

'We could go to Blossom Hall,' I said. 'The Whirtley woman mentioned something about tea. And if we don't like the Interesting Project we can always wangle out of it.'

'If we go,' said Ann, 'we'll be in it up to the neck.'

'*You* don't have to come,' I said. 'I'll get somebody else.'

Actually I wanted Ann to come with me more than anybody, and I had a feeling that her sense of curiosity would make her come, especially if I suggested that she needn't, and I was right.

'Oh, I'll come,' she said. 'If you can bear it, I can.'

'It might be jolly good,' I said hopefully. 'She might be going to offer us the use of her parkland for practice gallops. That would be super! She may have had it revealed to her in a dream that she ought to take all the poor little ponies off the road and give them some lovely parkland to gallop in. She may be frightfully rich and burning to do something for the cause of equitation.'

Ann said gloomily that she was quite sure there would be a catch in it.

'She probably wants us to do a flag day,' she said, 'and you know I never dare ask people to buy flags. I did it for the orphans, and I just slunk into a doorway and got nothing, and Daddy had to put five pounds into my box all in small change or I wouldn't have had anything at all.'

'OK,' I said. 'If it's a flag day we're out.'

Saturday came, and as I had predicted you couldn't tell that George had a scratch, though Mrs Derry still fussed about and said she was sure he was going to limp at any minute, and darling-do-be-careful.

Ann and I hacked to Moorside with our lunches, oats, grooming tools, and everything else we needed neatly packed up. We weren't particularly interested, so for once we hadn't that cold and hot sensation of excitement that one gets before a pony event. It was hot, so we wore our new shirts, mine was yellow and Ann's blue, and our well-brushed jodhpurs and boots, and we took our black coats for the Grand Parade and for going up for any cups we might win.

On the road we saw a lot of other people also making for Moorside, in fact there was a complete traffic block where some girl's pony was planted firmly broadside across the road and she had no idea how to pull or push it round. Nobody else seemed to have much idea either, in fact Ann had to get down and encourage the pony to move, which he did, recognising the hand and voice of experience. The girl remounted, and Ann gave the pony a whack, and the girl lost her stirrups and went on to his neck.

'Golly,' she said as she came back to me. 'Most of these people look as if they were on a pony for the first time in history.'

'Don't criticise the entry until after the competition,' I said, and she said, 'Well, look at them. I ask you!'

We reached the ground, which was merely a large field belonging to a farm, and decided that the whole thing was rather crude. The ring was not fenced but was made by running a rope round some stakes, and there were a few benches for spectators but no proper seats. There was a Scoutish kind of tent marked Stewards, and a St John Ambulance tent with a nurse standing by the flap looking hopeful. The ponies were on the far side of the field, and a few people were exercising up and down.

Ann and I went and joined them but found very few people there we knew. Besides ourselves there only seemed to be about half a dozen experienced riders, and the rest were obviously in for their first or second competition, and fond mothers were all over the place tying numbers on, in some cases upside down. One mother even held up a child's number to me and said, 'Where does this go?'

Ann said, 'Gosh, why did we come?' I said, to encourage the other entry, and she said would I kindly stop quoting out of books, as I had done nothing else since we left home.

The first class, for ponies under thirteen hands, was called into the collecting ring, and you should have seen the small kids scrambling about and backing into each other, while half the ponies were calmly cropping grass regardless of frenzied rein-pulling, and several others walked straight across the ring and out at the other side.

However, by then a few older and more experienced-looking people had begun to arrive, which we thought was a good thing as we hadn't liked the idea of snatching all the prizes from the hands of these babes.

I was mainly interested in the 14–2 showing class in which I had decided to show Rapide. He had not Black Boy's natural aptitude for showing, so I wanted him to get some practice and had given him a lot of schooling for this purpose. I thought Moorside would be a good small show for him to take a first or second, and it would give him confidence for bigger events. He looked beautifully groomed and sure of himself, and I patted his nose and said, 'Now you do as well as you did yesterday in the paddock, and we're home.'

Rapide made a face at me. He was given to making faces and I never quite knew what they meant. The only time he ever won me a cup he made a face at the woman who was presenting it, and she turned quite pale and nearly dropped it. She didn't understand Rapide, and probably thought he was about to take a bite out of her hat. Gosh, I was embarrassed.

However, to return to Moorside. I glanced over the other ponies in the 14–2 class as we waited to go into the ring, and there didn't look to be any frightening opposition, apart from Ann's George who was the sort of eye-catching pony with a long stride and dignified action beloved by certain judges, though George wasn't very light in hand and was apt to become unbalanced at critical moments.

There was a very neat farmer's daughter on a very neat pony. She looked frightfully serious and wore a dark blue coat. There was also a boy in a tweed hacking jacket on a long-backed bay, who looked so confident that for the first time I felt a twinge in my middle. Before I had time to see any more the ring steward called us in and we began riding round.

Now that Class Two was in action I saw that it was a more competent lot than I had expected. This shook me, and I had Rapide on rather a tight short rein which he resented. Hastily realising that he was inclined to overbend I let him walk out for a little and collected him. He went calmly into his trot and I felt that all was well at last.

In front of me Ann was riding George like the book, but so was everybody else riding like the book. I never saw such a lot of correct riding in my life. Nobody crowded anybody and nobody ran out. Then the ring steward told us to canter and things began to happen. A girl on a dashing pony whizzed past me, her pony bucked, and she came off. Two other people couldn't get their ponies to canter. One resorted to whacking and was stopped by the judge, the other just gave up trying and trotted on. I noticed that the farmer's daughter in dark blue was going beautifully, so was the boy on the long-backed bay and a few other people, in fact I was noticing the others to such an extent that for an instant I forgot it was Rapide I was riding and not Black Boy until to my dismay I found he was blithely cantering on the wrong leg. I tried to change him, but it was too late. He crowded George in front and for one humiliating moment I thought he was going to run out.

By the time I had collected him I saw that the neat dark blue girl had been called in, also the competent boy. Ann was called in third. Seeing my chances melt away like this completely upset me. Another boy was called in, and by now there was no opposition of any kind left and I was called fifth.

I had enough presence of mind to rein back well and Rapide obliged by standing squarely, but honestly by then I was so unsure of myself and of him that I found myself looking down to see what his legs were doing, and of course the judge's eye was on me as I did it, further jeopardising any chances I had left.

I sat quietly and watched the others do their shows. The neat little blue girl was terribly good, so was the boy. Ann's figure of eight didn't quite come off, and I could tell that she was a bit flustered at the way things had turned out after the way we had criticised other people before the show began.

The boy in fourth place was called Leonard Payne and was one of Mrs Darcy's pupils. He wasn't particularly good and I could not bear the thought of being beaten by him. Such, however, was to be my fate on this dark day of my history. Leonard had practised his show many times under Mrs Darcy's eye and it went off beautifully.

It was my turn. I walked a circle, trotted, cantered slowly, came back to a trot, then cantered on the other leg. It seemed to go all right, only Rapide was obviously not happy. I went back to my place and dragged off the saddle, and by now I felt so dim and low that I wouldn't have been surprised if the judge had found saddle galls or anything else on Rapide.

However, he made the usual vague muttering sounds and told me to lead out in hand at a walk and trot back. This went off quite decently and I hoped it was not too late.

The judge then told the first five to walk round in a circle, showing that he was not yet satisfied with the placing. While we did this I tried to sum up my chances. There was still hope. Ann was moved from third to second, displacing the tweed boy, and I could not think I would not displace Leonard Payne and get the Reserve (which was bad enough when I had foolishly counted on being first or second). But they called us in, and there was I, still fifth and unclassed, and the rosettes were given out. I retired feeling very dim indeed.

The next class we were interested in was of course the fourteen-and-under jumping. Showing the state of conceit we were in when we arrived, I must confess that we had both been certain of getting clear rounds.

We didn't get clear rounds! Actually we tied for third place with four faults each. By now we were both thoroughly snappy. Ann said that it was George's scratch that was to blame, and I said it was Rapide's bad luck to be having an off day, but the truth was as we very well knew that we had started off much too confident and careless and that is fatal in riding. One should be just as keyed-up at a small affair as a big one.

'Here I go!' said Ann grimly as we rode out of the ring. 'Second at Chatton Show last Saturday against some real riders, and third at Moorside today among a lot of kids from riding schools.'

'Oh, dry up!' I barked, not liking to have my rash words thrown back at me. 'We certainly shan't be needing our black coats to ride up for cups, and strange as it may seem, not having won any firsts we shan't be invited to ride in the Grand Parade.'

Just for something to do we went in for the Musical Chairs, and I was first and Ann second, though that didn't soothe us much. We fed the ponies and gave them drinks, and after partly quenching our own misery with about six ices each we rode home. I knew Mummy would merely shrug her shoulders and say, 'Nobody wins all the time,' whereas Mrs Derry would probably weep copiously over Ann and nearly let all the blinds down, being that sort of mother. I was sorry for Ann's young sister Pam, because I knew she would never hear the end of that scratch she let George get.

It had been a shocking day, and I have told you all about it because it served us jolly well right for thinking we were too good for Moorside. It taught me a lesson, and I have never since thought I was too good for anything, so I hope you will not do so either, however good you may be.

5 My rash deed

Being the summer holidays, I went up to the riding school for the weekly cross-country ride, and as we all clattered out of the gate a dark shadow flitted across the hedge and somebody's pony side-stepped and bucked.

Wendy Mead rode up and said, 'What's happening here?' Then she said, 'Oh, it's that awful Dean child. Get away with you! And don't come round here again, slinking in hedges.'

I saw then it was Dinah Dean, and she gave me a longing look, but I looked the other way. We went for our ride, and it was wonderful, over Neshbury Common and through the pinewood glades, and we did a bit of hedge-jumping and the sort of things you do in Handy Hunter competitions. But all the time I had a weird feeling about Dinah that I couldn't shake off. Don't get the idea that I am a Noble Character, in fact if you have read my other books you will already be saying Far From It, but it seemed to be a slur on the glorious cause of equitation that a person without any money to pay for it should want a lesson so badly that she would cheat a riding school to get it. And as you know, if you have survived after reading my aforesaid earlier books, the cause of equitation is the main object of my life. I felt as if I ought to Do

Something About It, but I didn't know what, and I didn't want to bother anyway.

When I got home Mummy was out, and Mrs Crosby had gone home, so I made myself a beaker of cocoa and a pile of toast, and brought all my tack into the kitchen to clean it, which in the ordinary way I am not allowed to do, as when I have finished there seems to be Brasso and saddle-soap all over the chairs, floor, etc. I took my time over getting everything clean, and then lugged it all back to the tack room and went upstairs.

In a box on the top of the cupboard where I hang my clothes were my very first check coat and jodhpurs, now much too small for me. They were secondhand when I bought them at an auction four years ago, but they were good quality and had been kept clean and mended, so there was lots of life in them yet for somebody small enough to wear them. Actually I was keeping them for my descendants in the hope that I would one day have some horsy daughters, but now I told myself hastily that any daughters I might have would probably be quite unlike me, and very earnest about fossils or Alsatians or ballet and have no use for riding things, and I would be sorry I had kept them for such unworthy creatures.

I bundled the things under my arm, wrote a note for Mummy saying 'Back for supper', and stuck it on her typewriter, so that if – as usual – she came back bursting with inspiration for a new chapter of *Basil the Bird-Song Boy* (which was the off-putting title of the new book she had begun to write) she couldn't fail to see it.

Then I got out my bike and dashed off to the new estate where all the houses were the same, and just like the houses that children of three draw, boxes with lids and flat fronts.

I asked a kid where the Deans lived, and she showed me the house. It looked even horrider than the others as it wasn't very clean and there was a lopsided blind upstairs.

I knocked at the door and Dinah answered it. Before she had time to fall down dead with shock, I shoved the parcel at her and muttered, 'Here, these are for you, and perhaps someday you'll be able to get some riding lessons.'

Then I dashed off before she could thank me or anything. When one does a deed like this one is supposed to glow with happiness, but I must say I didn't. I only began to think that probably the noble cause of equitation would have got along just as well if I had kept my coat and jodhs for my descendants as I had originally intended, especially if one of my daughters turned out to be horsy after all, as she very well might, because of course I should do all I could to put her off fossils and Alsatians and ballet while she was a helpless infant.

So I felt that as usual I had been quite mad, and that Mummy was right when she said you should never do anything drastic in cold blood. Or was it hot blood? Anyway, I'd done it, and I couldn't go and snatch the things back, so I started thinking about something else which happened to be Mrs Whirtley, and wondering if Ann would prove to be right about the flag day and if so, how we could get out of it.

I arrived home, and Mummy asked where had

I been, and I said nowhere – as one does – and after supper I took Rapide into the little paddock behind the orchard and gave him some very intensive schooling indeed, because I was so annoyed with him over Moorside.

I kept him at the slow trot, then changed gradually to an extended trot, and back to slow. Then I rode some circles, and crossed my stirrups and trotted again. Then I rode him at the loose rein walk and the ordinary walk, and tried a quarter turn to either side, and put him through a complete imaginary show. Believe me, he did everything beautifully – as he would when it didn't matter – and looked at me as much as to say 'I know I'm good.' I said, 'Well, why did you let me down on Saturday?' I felt furious, but patted him all the same for doing well, which a pony naturally expects, and took him in and rubbed him down and gave him his supper.

The next evening Mummy had some letters to post and said she would walk down to the post office with them as the box in our lane is a bit unpredictable.

She had been gone ten minutes when there was a knock at the door. I was reading the new copy of *Riding* which Mrs Lowe kindly passes on to me, so I didn't like to have to uncoil myself or break off in an exciting bit about stable management.

On the doorstep stood a person in a neat coat and jodhpurs. Mine! It was Dinah Dean.

She blurted out, 'I never thanked you for these. I was so stunned. It was marvellous of you. I don't know how to thank you. I mean – '

'That's all right,' I said, running my eye over her. Apart from the decent coat and jodhs she looked frightful. She had on some very scruffy shoes and the same washed-out pink tee-shirt, and her hair was more lopsided than ever.

I said, 'If you don't mind me saying so, you ought to wear a shirt with a collar and tie, and couldn't you shove your hair back and stick a grip in?'

She went bright red and said, 'I'm s-sorry.'

'Look, you'd better come upstairs,' I said, feeling like slaying her but somehow driven on by my Better Feelings. 'I've got a white shirt that's too small for me and I can probably find you an old tie and some grips.'

She followed me up to my room, and when I opened the door she said, 'Ooooh!'

My room did look smashing. On the tallboy were my cups and prizes (which I happened to have cleaned that morning) and all round the room was my Pony Frieze. This frieze consists of a green line which I painted right round the walls about four feet from the ground, and all along it are stuck pictures of horses cut out of magazines, standing on the green line or prancing along it as though it were the grass in a paddock. There was just about a yard of the line without any horses because I still hadn't got enough to fill it up.

'Oh, it's wonderful!' said Dinah, and rushed up to the frieze and started patting the horses with her finger.

'What a lovely idea.'

'It's not bad,' I said.

She said, 'I've got an old *Country Life* that Daddy brought home wrapped round something. It's got pictures of horses in it. I'll bring it for you, for the unfinished bit.'

I said rather squashingly that she needn't bother, I could get some myself. Then I found the old shirt and said, 'It isn't too clean but you can wash it.' I found an old fawn tie too that had gone stringy, and about six grips. Dinah looked as if she was going to have a fit, and started muttering thank you about a million times, but I wanted to get rid of her and get back to *Riding*, and anyway Doing Good always makes me feel hot and bothered, so I bundled her downstairs.

'Now look,' I said. 'You buzz off and don't come here again. I don't want you.'

'Oh, please could I come and muck out your stable?' she said. 'I'd come every morning before I get Daddy's breakfast. I'd like to, because you gave me all these things.'

'No, you can't,' I said. 'I just don't want you here! Can't you understand?'

She said, 'Well, do you think I could go and muck out Mrs Darcy's stable? I feel so awful about what I did. I didn't mean to cheat.'

'I know you didn't,' I said. 'But I advise you to keep away from Mrs Darcy's or you'll be well and truly slain. Now go away, and stay away, if you can understand plain English.'

She got the idea and gave a sort of gulp, so I shoved her out and shut the door thankfully. I had been terrified that Mummy would come back before the kid was gone.

Next morning when I went down to unlock my tack room I found someone had been there before me. It had all been tidied up to such an extent it nearly hurt you to look at it. I know my tack room usually looks as though a tornado has gone through it, but the point is that when it is in a muddle I know just where to put my hand on everything and when it is tidy – although it looks good – I can't find a thing. On the bench was a note which read, 'I got through the window. I hope you don't mind. Dinah.'

I wrote on the bottom of the note, 'Yes, I do mind, and it'll take me ages to get the place back into the kind of muddle I like, so if you come back here again, buzz off. Jill.'

The last thing I wanted was to get mixed up with Dinah Dean. I don't think she came back. The note stayed where it was.

6 Blossom Hall

Ann and I were a long time making up our minds what to wear to go to Mrs Whirtley's.

'The point is, are we going to ride there?' said Ann.

I said, 'Of course we are. Otherwise we shall have to go in school-ish cotton frocks and look like a couple of kids. The point is, shall we wear just shirts and jodhpurs as it's rather hot weather, or our tweed coats, or our blacks?

Ann said our blacks would be too hot. I said, yes, but jolly sophisticated, and it was better to make Mrs Whirtley think we were a couple of hard women to hounds than just two more child riders, and anyway if we put some of Mummy's powder on our faces it would stop the hotness showing through.

Eventually we decided on our black coats. We plastered on the powder, and a lipstick called Flame-Thrower that Ann found at the local chemist's, but we had to rub a lot of that off as it was rather frightening.

We started off early on Black Boy and George, and rode slowly so as not to arrive practically on fire.

Blossom Hall was a great big shabby Georgian mansion with wonderful parkland all round it, and a lawn in front that looked about a mile square.

Ann said, 'Think of living in a place like this and being able to ride round the park all day. Some people are jolly lucky.'

'If ever I'm rich,' I said, 'this is what I'll buy, but I never will be.'

Ann said we might both marry millionaires and I said, 'Don't be so feeble,' and she said, well somebody had to marry millionaires and it might as well be us.

Then Mrs Whirtley came down the imposing steps and said, 'Come along, girls. Welcome to Blossom Hall.'

We rather liked the look of her, because actually she was exactly like a horse about the face, even to the forelock and big teeth.

We tied the ponies where she showed us, and went into a large drawing-room full of big bouncing settees and oil paintings and looped-up curtains, where four other people of about our age were sitting round. Two of them were boys in shirts and trousers, and the others were girls in cotton dresses and sandals. They looked at Ann and me rather awesomely as if we were grown-ups. Nobody said anything and we all sat there feeling dumb. Soon five more people arrived, three boys and two girls, and then another girl who was in a black coat . . . with large round specs and long plaits. She glared at Ann and me.

Mrs Whirtley said, 'Now we're all here. To business, I think, don't you, people?'

As none of us knew what the business was we all looked quite blank, and one girl giggled out loud.

Mrs Whirtley had a very fluty voice and kept patting the side of her nose while she was talking.

I daren't look at her for fear of having hysterics. She said, 'Well now, people, I must tell you why I asked you to come here.'

('Flag Day!' Ann muttered.)

'We have just come to live at this wonderful old house with its fine park, and I feel that some good use should be made of it.'

('Shouldn't think it is,' I muttered back.)

'Mr Whirtley and I feel that it is up to us to make a real effort for some good cause – '

('There you are!' muttered Ann.)

' – and this park and garden will make a wonderful setting for the kind of effort we have in mind.'

('Shut up, you're off the beam!' I muttered back.)

'What we are thinking of,' said Mrs Whirtley, 'is a kind of fête, and that is why you riders are here today, because the fête is to be in aid of various societies for the protection and care of horses, and we propose to hold it next month, on the second Saturday in September, just before you all go back to school.'

I began to brighten up a bit.

'I have always been of the opinion,' went on Mrs Whirtley, 'that young people have the best and brightest ideas, so I decided to form my committee from people like yourselves, representing young horse lovers from various parts of the county. Are you all willing to be on my committee and help me to arrange the fête?'

Everybody looked at everybody else and nobody said anything, we were all paralysed.

'Oh, don't be shy,' said Mrs Whirtley, and the girl with specs and plaits grinned rather sickeningly and said, 'I think we're all willing, Mrs Whirtley.'

She said, 'Splendid, splendid!' and beamed, and went on, 'Now what you have to decide is what we are going to do at the fête. Don't think about the food or anything like that because that is my affair. But if we get a thousand people here, how are we going to amuse them? It's got to be lively and appealing to everybody of all ages. Now, let me hear some of your ideas.'

To my horror she looked straight at me and I wished I hadn't made myself look so sophisticated. I sucked off a bit of my lipstick and it tasted awful.

'Do tell me your name,' said Mrs Whirtley.

'Jill Crewe,' I said.

'Oh, of course, I've heard a lot about Jill Crewe. Well, come along, Jill, what do you suggest we do at the fête?'

'C-could we have a pageant?' I stuttered feebly. 'Ponies Through the Ages, or something?'

'That's one idea,' said Mrs Whirtley. 'A pageant. Anything else?'

One kid chirped up that her mother had a Queen Elizabeth dress, so she would like to ride her pony and be Queen Elizabeth in the pageant.

'Well, dear, we haven't got as far as that,' said Mrs Whirtley, looking very snootily at the kid who went a sort of pale green. 'Any more ideas? What about you?' And she looked at the girl with specs, who promptly said her name was Clarissa Dandleby, and what about a point-to-point?

Mrs Whirtley looked a bit stunned, as well she might, and said, 'Of course, dear, we're not all point-to-point riders,' and Clarissa Dandleby said she had ridden in her first point-to-point when she was only eleven and hoped she would soon be steeplechasing, and Mrs Whirtley said, 'I think we'd better not have *too* big ideas,' and Clarissa said, 'Well, what about some Hunter Trials?'

'Couldn't we have just an ordinary gymkhana?' said a boy, and Clarissa Dandleby glowered at him and said, 'How jolly tame,' and another boy said, 'Well, let's have a gymkhana *and* Hunter Trials *and* a pageant,' and about five people said 'Gosh!'

'I do think,' said Mrs Whirtley, 'that perhaps a gymkhana would be the best idea. It lets everybody in, doesn't it? Even the tinies.'

'Of course, if it's going to be a kids' thing – ' began somebody, and Clarissa Dandleby interrupted, 'It wouldn't be too bad if we could have dressage and cross-country too.'

'Oh that's much too ambitious,' said Mrs Whirtley.

'I want to be in a pageant,' said the kid who wanted to be Queen Elizabeth.

'I want to be Dick Turpin,' said another kid.

'Couldn't we have an open jumping event?' suggested Ann, 'and get some famous riders and horses to enter?'

'I'm afraid that might cost so much to organise that it would swallow up all the profits,' said Mrs Whirtley, 'and after all we do want to make a lot of money for the needy horses.'

'Couldn't we do a play?' said a very fat girl in a too-tight cotton dress. 'I could write one. I've written about eight plays. One's called *With Drake on the High Seas*, only I could alter it a bit and call it *With Saddle in the Sierras* or something like that.'

'Your plays are mouldy,' said the boy sitting next

to her who looked like her brother. 'They did one at your school and everybody was nearly sick.'

'That isn't very kind, dear,' said Mrs Whirtley, and the boy said, 'Well, Moira's plays *are* mouldy. I wouldn't mind doing a play if it could be a decent play like *Murder on the Stairs* or an Agatha Christie one.'

'If a play's in the open air it might as well be a pageant,' said somebody else, and everybody yelled, 'Now we're back at the pageant again!'

'I'll tell you what we'll do,' said Mrs Whirtley, 'we'll have tea, and meanwhile you can all be thinking and then we'll have some brilliant ideas.'

I must say the tea cheered us all up no end, it was simply smashing. There were four kinds of sandwiches, and buns and meringues and jam puffs and chocolate cake. Mrs Whirtley proved to be the most decent kind of hostess and didn't pass the best things just once but several times, and there was enough for everybody to have about three of everything if they wanted.

However, her hopes must have been dashed to the ground, because far from developing any brilliant ideas after tea nobody could think of anything new to say, except a frightful kid with a lisp who said, 'couldn't there be a fanthy dreth parade with decorated ponieth?'

Most people turned pale green at the idea, but one person said, 'I think fancy dress would be a good idea, and we could have collecting boxes and shake them at people and get a lot of money. We could dress up like pirates.'

'I know! We could sell pirate flags!' yelled some

ghastly-minded boy. Ann and I looked at each other and shuddered.

'I have already decided,' said Mrs Whirtley. 'We shall have a gymkhana. It isn't very original, but it appeals to everybody and we may be able to get some good riders for open jumping.'

Clarissa Dandleby gave a snort, and said that Mrs Whirtley simply wouldn't get anybody who was any good to come for an ordinary gymkhana.

'My dear child,' said Mrs Whirtley in a blistering voice, 'I don't remember your name, but let me tell you that I have been getting up gymkhanas for years and I have never yet had to complain about the attendance.'

'Squash for Clarissa,' muttered a girl behind me. 'She thinks she's the best-known girl rider in the county.'

Somebody said, could there be a novice hack class, as she had a novice hack she wanted to enter, and Mrs Whirtley said there could be.

She then added, 'The tickets will be printed in a couple of days and I shall send them out to you. I want you each to sell two dozen to start with.

Ann made a face at me, but everybody seemed quite satisfied except Clarissa Dandleby who, in spite of her squash, still went on muttering that simply nobody would come to a gymkhana unless there was a dressage test and open jumping with large prizes, and as for her she couldn't be expected to compete along with a lot of kids on ponies.

That was the end of the meeting, and we wandered out on the drive and sorted out our ponies who by now had all made friends and got their ropes mixed.

Clarissa's pony was a lovely dark chestnut mare with four white socks, and Clarissa did a lot of frantic kicking before she got away at an extremely uncollected canter. She was obviously the kicking type.

7 We *must* sell tickets

'About these awful two dozen tickets that we've each got to sell,' I said a few days later, sitting rather uncomfortably on a turned-up box, watching Ann give a lesson to her young sister.

'I've just realised why Pam's so ghastly,' she said. 'She doesn't ride at all. She just sits and uses her hands.'

'She's what they call a passive rider,' I said. 'Tell her to use her legs and seat.'

'I have,' said Ann. 'She won't.'

'Well, cross her stirrups and make her.'

'She'll fall off.'

'Well, let her,' I said. 'What are we going to do about selling these tickets?'

Ann told Pam that she could get down and added, 'I think you're absolutely hopeless.'

I pointed out that she shouldn't tell people that, because all the books on equitation said that the pupil must be encouraged until a spirit of accord was established between man and horse.

Ann said she couldn't care less, and went on, 'I'm not having the ponies out again till it stops raining. I'm sick of cleaning sodden tack and drying ponies after every ride.'

'You might suggest something about these awful

tickets,' I said. 'I mean, two dozen *each* – '

'Oh, it's not too bad,' said Ann. 'I'll sell Mummy about four, and about ten to people in our form, and Diana and James – that's two more – and Mrs Darcy will buy one for herself and one each for Wendy and Joey – '

'Gosh!' I said. 'You have a nerve. Half those people are mine, anyway. If you sell one to Diana then I ought to sell one to James, and as for Mrs Darcy, it's a bit much to think you can bag her *and* Wendy *and* Joey.'

Ann said, 'Twenty-four times two pounds fifty works out at sixty pounds. We'd better have a Bring and Buy Sale after all and raise enough money to pay for our own tickets.'

'Let's go and see some people,' I said. 'Now, before we rub down the ponies. Let's walk up to their doors dragging sodden ponies and looking pathetic and ask them to buy a ticket for downtrodden horses. That ought to shake them.'

Ann said, where should we start? and I said, what about her next-door neighbour? and she said that wasn't fair, as Mrs Ponsford was practically hers and would have to buy one from her anyway.

'You old Scrooge,' I said. 'All right, let's go along *my* road and start at Mrs Norton's. Come on.'

We oozed up Mrs Norton's drive and knocked at the door. The rain was pouring off our riding hats and down the necks of our macs, and the ponies were plastered with mud and looked extremely downtrodden. We didn't look at all nice.

Mrs Norton came to the door, and I said, 'Oh, would you like to buy some tickets for a – '

'No, thank you,' said Mrs Norton very sweetly, and shut the door.

'Help!' said Ann. 'It's *worse* than a flag day.'

'Well, let's try the next house,' I suggested. 'We're so wet already that a bit more doesn't matter.'

We toiled up the drive to West Lea, and the housekeeper said Mrs Jones was out, so we toiled down again, and the ponies made snorting noises expressing their fed-up-ness, and I could feel the rain coming inside my mac, which was depressing as I couldn't see Mummy buying me a new one if I wanted to hunt in the winter.

'Let's go to Mrs Pugh's,' I said, 'and if we don't sell any there let's throw them away and not go to Mrs Whirtley's any more.'

Strangely enough, Mrs Pugh bought three tickets, and as we rode back under the dripping trees we argued about who had sold the odd one.

'It's mine,' I said. 'I asked her, the minute she opened the door.'

Ann pointed out that it was she who had said what the ticket was for.

'OK,' I said. 'Call it three pounds seventy-five each. Let's go home, because it's going to take hours to rub the ponies down and clean the tack and we'll never get a polish on it.'

When I got to our cottage Mrs Crosby was in one of her worst moods and said I was for ever filling her kitchen with dirty sopping wet saddles, and I said I didn't make the weather, and she said, if I was her girl she'd find me something better to do, and so we went on and on as we had done a thousand times before.

It cleared up for Saturday, and we went to a Horse Show at Mitby, and Ann's father let us use the horse box and travel properly, so we arrived dustless and smart with everything polished and the ponies looking super.

This show was divided into two parts. There was a dressage and cross-country event, and also a gymkhana.

We watched the dressage and wondered if we would ever be good enough to go in for it, or if we could get somebody to coach us. Then we entered for one or two of the gymkhana events, and I won the potato race, mainly because everybody else was cockeyed and couldn't get within miles of the bucket, and my potatoes must have been a better shape than usual because I hurled them madly about and they went in, so I wasn't too proud of my achievement.

Ann was a certainty for the Bending until she was beaten in the final heat by a girl who missed out two poles, and the judge didn't even notice, which didn't say much for him.

We had had enough, so we went back to the main ring to see the end of the cross-country, and I shoved my red rosette into my pocket because I was a bit ashamed of what I had won it for. There is something definitely sordid about potatoes when all around you are magnificent people who do dressage tests on blood ponies.

'Look over there,' said Ann. 'It's Captain Cholly-Sawcutt.'

The famous British Team rider was surrounded by a small crowd of friends and admirers, and as usual he looked very friendly and jovial, and a bit like royalty look on grand public occasions.

'I'll tell you what,' I said suddenly. 'I'm going to ask him to buy a ticket for the Whirtley massacre.'

'You can't!' said Ann with a yell of horror.

'Yes, I can. After all, I did give his fat daughters a riding lesson while Mrs Darcy was away' – (this happened in a previous book of mine) – 'and he rode Petronelle round our jumps, and signed our autograph books.'

'He won't remember you,' said Ann. 'Look at all those terrific people he's with, judges, and the hunting crowd and everything. You can't!'

If I had thought about it in cold blood I don't think I could, but I just pushed a few ends of hair under my hat, and picked a bit of hay off my coat, and rubbed my boots on the backs of my jodhs, and marched across to where the great man stood, and gave a cough.

At first he didn't notice me, and then by a bit of luck he turned round and practically fell over me.

After we had both reeled about and got on our feet again, he said, 'If it isn't Jill Crewe!'

I felt so bucked that he had actually remembered my name that I went a sort of boiled colour, especially as all the famous people around had been looking at me as if I was something too mere for words.

'Having a good time?' said the great man in a very friendly way.

'Terrific,' I said.

'Won anything yet?'

'Well, not actually – ' I began, going redder than ever, and just at that moment I dragged my hands

out of my pockets where I usually keep them when
I don't know what to do with them, and out came
that awful red rosette and fell plop on the emerald
turf, and a very noble-looking man in immaculate
tweeds stooped down and handed it back to me in
an impressed kind of way.

'Nice work,' said Captain Cholly-Sawcutt.
'Honestly, I didn't notice you in the dressage.'

'It's for the potato race,' I blurted, and there was
one solid yell of laughter. I felt ghastly.

'Well, it takes a good eye to win a potato race,' said
the great man pleasantly. 'I bet you I couldn't win
one. How's that good pony you rode in the Hunter
Trials last spring?'

'Rapide?' I said. 'He's not too bad. But what
I wanted was – I mean to say, do you know
the Whirtleys at Blossom Hall? Because they're
having a fête in aid of charities for horses, and
I've got to sell twenty-four tickets, and honestly
I never shall, it's practically a physical impossibil-
ity, but oh, Captain Cholly-Sawcutt, do you think
you could possibly bear to buy one? Because if
you do everybody else would buy one too.' Having got this out I stood there looking completely
screwy.

'I hope they're not fifty pounds each, or anything like that,' said the Captain, smiling at one
or two of his superlatively horsy friends. 'This
girl,' he added, meaning me, 'could get away with
anything.'

'They're two pounds fifty,' I said, 'and I believe
there's going to be a jolly good tea.'

'That settles it,' he said. 'Give me a dozen.'

I nearly passed out.

'Sorry,' he said, 'is that too many?'

'Gosh!' I said. 'Thirty pounds. It's terrific. Oh, I say, it is decent of you.'

'How many do you want to sell?' he said.

'Oh, another dozen,' I said, mentally deciding with great presence of mind that Ann would then be able to foist hers off on to Mummy and all the rest of my intended customers.

'Done!' said the Captain. 'It's a deal. Come on, Colonel, take a dozen tickets for a fête in aid of horses. That'll be the best thing you ever did in the cause of equitation since you got twenty-four faults at Richmond Horse Show in 1904.'

'I repudiate your insults,' said the Colonel, 'but I'll pay for the tickets.' (I looked up 'repudiate' after in the dictionary and decided to use it myself later, as I like a new word.)

Dumbly I folded the ten pound notes which were handed to me and put them in the pocket of my jodhs all mixed up with the potato rosette. When I became conscious again, I said, 'Thanks. Thanks most frightfully. I'll post the tickets to you the minute I get home.'

When I got back to Ann she didn't believe me. She thought I was making it up until I showed her the ten pound notes. Then she said, 'Well, while you were at it you might have sold them another dozen. That would have got rid of a few of mine too.'

'What colossal nerve!' I said. 'You can have all my customers now, Mummy and the Lowes and Mrs Darcy's crowd and everybody.'

So she calmed down, and I swaggered across the trodden, warm-smelling turf swishing the tail of my best black coat, and soon we got to the horse box and watched Ann's father's man leading the happy ponies up the ramp, and I felt very thrilled and decided that even if it meant never having another Christmas present as long as I lived I would have a black coat and boots next Christmas.

When I got home and told Mummy all about it, to my surprise she put on one of her non-co-operative looks.

'I don't know that I approve of it, Jill. You put Captain Cholly-Sawcutt into a position in which he couldn't do anything but buy your tickets. I don't think it was very sportsmanlike.'

'But if he hadn't liked it,' I pointed out, 'he needn't have bought a whole dozen and made his friend buy another dozen. He could have bought just one or two.'

'You seem to have an answer for everything,' said Mummy, 'but I do hate people who thrust themselves forward, and thank goodness it is something you have never done, so don't start it now.'

I went upstairs to put the two dozen tickets in an envelope for Captain Cholly-Sawcutt, and I wrote a note saying, 'I hope you don't think I pushed these on you and it was dreadful cheek, because I didn't mean it like that, and if you do, send the tickets back and I'll send you the sixty pounds.'

Then I came downstairs feeling better, and blow me down! Mummy had discovered the potato race rosette which had fallen out of the pocket of my jodhpurs and had some bits of dusty straw sticking to it, and she was much more thrilled than she need have been, and after all the prize was only ten pounds, but I had earned it myself and that always meant a lot to Mummy.

8   In the cause of equitation

When I went up to the riding school for my lesson Mrs Darcy was very excited to hear about Mrs Whirtley's fête. Being August it was fairly quiet up there, as a lot of people were away at the seaside, and only the keen ones who didn't want to miss any of the shows were going as usual for their lessons. Normally Mrs Darcy was so busy that she had a waiting list of people who wanted lessons, and she was so popular that no other teacher stood a chance at all. Also, practically every child for miles around now rode. People's mothers – including my own – used to talk about 'when this pony craze dies down', but I didn't see it dying down in my lifetime.

As you know, ponies have a spell of jumping perfectly and then all of a sudden get the idea of taking off too soon, or going spectator-shy or something like that. This is known as temperament. Rapide was off his jumping, and I thought it must in some way be my fault, because if you are a serious rider you should always blame yourself before you blame your pony, so I was putting in some hard work on him, under Mrs Darcy's eye.

I never got tired of her jumps or the neat look of her stables and well-kept ponies, and since some of my friends and I had practically run the place during its owner's absence – as I related in a previous book – I always had a feeling about the riding school that it partly belonged to me.

'It ought to be a good show,' said Mrs Darcy. 'Mrs Whirtley is a first-rate organiser and does things on a big scale.'

I told her about how I had sold the tickets to Captain Cholly-Sawcutt, and asked, 'Do you think there's a chance he might come? If he does, and jumps Petronelle for an exhibition, we'd need a tank regiment to keep the people away. It would be jolly good for the fête.'

'I don't think there's a hope of him being there,' she said. 'He'll be away, jumping with the British team, possibly on the Continent. But he might give his tickets to some of his friends and persuade them to enter for the open jumping. That's such a big attraction, if you can get well-known riders and horses.'

'If only he would,' I said.

'Tell you what,' said Mrs Darcy, 'I'll mention it to him myself. He's such a good sport. You haven't seen his place, have you? Marvellous training stables – breaking young horses – dressage – hunters – everything. Just your cup of tea.'

'Gosh!' I said with a sigh. 'I'm as likely to see the inside of Buckingham Palace.'

'Tell you what,' said Mrs Darcy again, 'if you say there's a class for novice hacks, how about you showing Sandy Two for me?'

I blinked several times. I had never dreamed in my wildest dreams – and believe me, some of my horsy dreams are extremely wild – of being asked

to show a horse out of Mrs Darcy's stable. I came
to earth when she made the blighting remark 'You
needn't if you don't want to.'

'Want to!' I yelled. 'Help! I'm not good enough.'

'That's up to you,' said Mrs Darcy. 'It's time you
stopped thinking you're a beginner. I'll give you the
necessary coaching if you'll struggle up here in your
spare time.'

'Actually I don't have any,' I said, 'but I'll make
some, even if it's in the stilly watches of the night.'

'Come and have a look at the fellow,' she said.

Sandy Two was out at grass in the little paddock
behind her bungalow. He was a roan of fifteen
hands, with black points, a lovely head, and large,
intelligent eyes.

'I'd love to show him,' I said, 'if you think I could
do him justice.'

'Don't worry,' said Mrs Darcy. 'Come up tomorrow night about eight and I'll run over what you need
to know.'

I went home feeling very excited, and dreamed
that night that I was showing Sandy Two and his
legs were getting longer and longer, and I couldn't
even mount him, and somebody picked me up with
a crane and put me in the saddle, and I tried to rein
back and Sandy Two sat down on the judge who
turned out to be my form teacher. She shouted,
'Remember what happens to people who think they
can ride horses too big for them!' I thought of a girl
at my school called Susan Pyke, whom I will not
call a friend, who in theory saw herself at her best
on something about sixteen hands but in practice
finished up in every collecting ring swinging on

her horse's neck like a monkey and arguing with the judge!

Was I glad to wake up!

After all this I thought it was time that Ann and I got busy boosting the fête, so we decided to go and see all the people from school who weren't on holiday. We went first to see two friends of ours called Val and Jackie Heath (whose actual names were Valerie and Jacqueline, only they had had the good sense to abandon these by the time they were about three).

Val and Jackie had been doing very well with their riding lately, in fact being lucky enough to have a horsy aunt in London they had ridden at Windsor Horse Show and Jackie had taken a first on one of her aunt's ponies in the 13–2 class. It had rather turned her head and given her ideas of grandeur, and even Val had bathed in the reflected glory and had never been quite the same since. Also Jackie had got David Broome's autograph, and she kept it wrapped in silver paper in a cigar box, and only showed it to special people.

The Heaths were quite glad to see us, and when we had had some lemonade and buns we had to stand for ages watching Val doing half-passes until we were nearly screaming, especially as Jackie said that their father was going to arrange for them to have some coaching in dressage from a man who had been trained in Italy by a man who had been a cavalry officer.

'Well, what about this fête?' I said at last, when I could get a word in. 'You'll both come, won't you? I mean,' I added sarkily, 'if it doesn't interfere with you jumping at Wembley, or anything like that.'

It is funny how some people never know when you are being sarky. Jackie said, 'Oh, we're not riding at Wembley, at least not this year,' and Ann said, 'Really? I'm frightfully surprised, but at least it will give the others a chance.' Then Val chased us both round their yard (living at a farm they have lots of room) and nearly laid me out with a dandy brush which caught me on the ear, and we all finished up by crashing into the door of a shed where there was a sick calf that had to have absolute quiet, and the door gave way and Ann sat down practically on the calf, and Mr Heath came out and was livid.

'You can buy two tickets from Ann,' I said when the noise of battle had died down.

'Is it just a gymkhana?' said Val. 'It sounds a bit tame.'

'No, it isn't just a gymkhana,' I said. 'It's a noble effort in the noble cause of noble equitation.'

'Gosh!' said Jackie. 'That's the first time I've ever known Jill to be short of adjectives.'

'I'm not short,' I told her witheringly, 'it's the only suitable adjective for anything so noble.'

'Oh, come on, be noble,' said Ann. 'Buy the tickets.'

Val said all right, they would buy two tickets and come if they could.

'You'll jolly well come,' I said. 'It's no good people buying tickets if nobody's going to be there on the day. And you'll jolly well enter for all the classes you can as soon as the schedules are out. Of course we understand that nobody else will stand a chance, but think what you'll be able to do with all that prize money.'

Again the sarcasm was wasted, as Jackie said seriously that it would be nice to buy some good hunting tack.

'Are you asking Susan Pyke?' she went on. 'I mean, she's always a bit of a sensation on one of her marvellous steeds, especially when she argues with the judges.'

Ann said that we'd better ask Susan, it always made one more, so we went along to her house. She was sitting in the garden, madly knitting, trying to finish a yellow polo-necked sweater, and was quite glad to see us.

'Daddy is buying me an Anglo-Arab mare,' she said when we told her about the fête. 'It would be a try-out for her, wouldn't it?'

'Oh, rather,' said Ann, 'and do get a lot of other people to come too.'

Susan promised that practically all her relations and friends would come to see her on the Anglo-Arab mare, and we said the more the merrier and she'd probably win everything hands down, and she said in a very Susan-ish way that she hoped the prizes were large, and I said in a rather sticky voice that this was a charity affair and its aim was rather to get money out of people than to give big prizes to the competitors, and Susan said she wouldn't mind that for just once, and she rather thought she'd enter for the open jumping and I said, do!

She couldn't have been nicer to us, if a bit condescending, and showed us how to do the neck of the polo-sweater so that it fitted and didn't look like a halter (as the ones I have knitted always do) and when we went away Ann said to me that

Susan would really be quite nice if she wasn't so sickening.

We toiled round all day getting people to promise to come to the fête, and we only hoped that everybody else on the committee was working as hard as we were, though we had our doubts about Clarissa Dandleby. I was so hot that when I got home all I could do was to totter into the larder and drink about a gallon of delicious orange fruit cup that was standing there. When Mummy came in I said brightly, 'I drank all the fruit cup, it was marvellous, it must have taken you ages to make with all that chopped fruit and mint and stuff,' and she said drily, 'It did, it took me about two hours to make it for three people who are coming in for a game of bridge tonight,' and I went cold with remorse. I mean, I just do these things and never think till it's too late. So I was peeling oranges and chopping apples and mint for ages after that, and my one consolation was that I hadn't noticed the sandwiches which were also ready for Mummy's bridge evening.

After all this I thought I was due for a little relaxation, so I got Black Boy out and went for a ride in the sunlit evening, all along the grass verges of the lanes. Birds in the trees were making the usual din they do make when they are going to bed, and as I watched the sinking sun I was so happy I wouldn't have changed places with anybody on earth.

9 Cecilia turns up

The next afternoon Mrs Whirtley rang up to say that there would be another meeting of the committee at her house on Tuesday afternoon, and she hoped I had been working hard, and would I mind letting Ann Derry know as it would save Mrs Whirtley a call as she had about a million to make.

Ann was in our cottage at the time, and she said at once, 'Whoopee! The tea the old girl gave us last time was what I call fantastic.'

'She won't keep it up,' I said. 'She'll let us down gently with weak orangeade and biscuits that have gone soft.'

Mummy chimed in that she thought we were the limit, and that working for a Cause was its own reward regardless of such earthly things as meringues, and I refrained from saying, 'That's what you think.'

Ann and I arrived at Blossom Hall, and soon we were all assembled in the drawing-room for the meeting, that is all except Clarissa Dandleby. I naturally hoped that she wasn't coming, as I had taken rather a dislike to her, but as though reading my anxious thoughts Mrs Whirtley said, 'We're all here except Clarissa Dandleby and she rang me up to say that she might be late, as she is coming by car and bringing a friend who would like to be on the committee.'

She had hardly finished speaking when a car was heard to stop outside, and Clarissa's somewhat foghornish voice was heard too, arguing with the driver about what time he was to come back for her. Then she came in and apologised for being late, but she had had to wait for her friend.

Then the friend came in and I practically collapsed.

It was my cousin Cecilia!

When I came round I found Cecilia sitting next to me with Clarissa in the row in front.

Cecilia said, 'Good gracious, Jill, what are you doing here? How on earth will the riding school manage without you?' and Clarissa turned round and looked at me through her enormous specs and said, 'Oh, do you run a riding school?' and I said, 'Of course not,' and Cecilia said, 'Oh, don't be so modest, Jill. You know you teach the sweet little kiddies to ride their dear little Shetlands and the nannies come too.'

Clarissa giggled, and I said nonchalantly, 'I'm starting a class for the under-twos, if you'd both like to join.'

Cecilia said, joking apart, she was quite surprised to see me on the committee, and I said, not as surprised as I was to see her as she was quite the most un-horsy person I knew, and she said one didn't have to be horsy to do Good Works, and in her set Good Works were all the thing just now, so she didn't care if it was worn-out

horses or suffering orphans or toothless Lithua-
nians.

Mrs Whirtley said, 'I see you two know each
other, how nice, but oughtn't we to get on with
the business?'

She then asked everybody what they had done
about boosting the fête and how many tickets they
had sold.

Ann and I were just thinking smugly that nobody
could have done as well as we had, when a boy got
up and said he had sold all his two dozen tickets on
the first day and had orders for four dozen more,
and a girl said, when were the gymkhana schedules
coming out, as twenty-three people she knew were
all dying to enter?

'Ah, the schedules!' said Mrs Whirtley. 'I've drawn
up what I think is a good list, and I'll read it to you
and then you can approve.'

A girl got up and said her mother wanted to know
if there could be a riding class for the under-sevens so
that her little brother could enter. He was only five
and so sweet and it would encourage him if he could
win a prize.

Mrs Whirtley looked a bit bleak and said there
would only be time for a few gymkhana events,
as there would only be the one ring for everything,
so she had planned just two classes for the younger
ones, Musical Chairs and Egg-and-Spoon for the
under-fourteens, and one showing class for ponies
and one for novice hacks, and one juvenile jumping
for under-sixteens. As there would be a big entry for
all these classes it would by then be the tea interval,
and after tea would be the open jumping. We would

be glad to know that she had already got some good
entries, including George Glee on Poetry, Bernard
Bushey on Charles Stewart, and Sonia Pretty on
How Now.

Everybody clapped, and when the clapping had
died down Cecilia got up and said, much as she
disliked appearing a wet blanket, there would be
people at the fête who might like to rest their
eyes from such a lot of horsy happenings, and
couldn't there be a marquee with an exhibition of
handicrafts and perhaps a competition for decorated
dinner tables?

Several people said, Help! and Mrs Whirtley said
that was quite an idea, only it would need somebody
good to organise it, and Cecilia said, 'Oh, I'll organise
it,' and Mrs Whirtley looked a bit winded and said,
'Thank you, dear.'

She then finished reading the schedule, and everybody approved – or if they didn't they daren't say so
– and Mrs Whirtley said she would get them off to
the printers, and would we let her know how many
we all wanted so that we could have them by the
weekend.

Clarissa Dandleby said darkly, 'I'm afraid you'll
be sorry, Mrs Whirtley, that you didn't take my
advice and have dressage and cross-country,' and
Mrs Whirtley said she thought she'd survive, and
after that it was time for tea.

The tea was, if anything, even better than before.
Cecilia chatted to me in a very friendly way, and said
did I remember the time I had stayed with her and
played with those awful children at the Rectory? I
said I remembered doing a lot of jolly hard work at

the Rectory, saving people's ponies from extinction, and she laughed and said, 'I do think you're weird.'

Just then a maid came in and said Miss Jill Crewe was wanted on the telephone. I started thinking of all the marvellous news I might be going to receive, but when I got to the phone it was Mummy.

She said, 'Is Cecilia there?' and when I said yes, and how did she know? she said that Aunt Primrose, Cecilia's mother, had rung up to say that Cecilia would be at Blossom Hall, and could I take her home with me for a few days?

I said, 'Oh!' in a strangled voice, and Mummy said she was sending a taxi at five o'clock for me and Cecilia and Cecilia's luggage, and perhaps Ann would be kind enough to take Black Boy home with her own pony.

I went back to the drawing-room and I said to Cecilia, 'You're coming home with me for a few days.' Cecilia said, 'How marvellous!' and I said, 'And I don't want any funny jokes about riding schools,' and she said, 'You *are* touchy. If you'd been at my school they'd have knocked all that out of you.' I said I couldn't think of a worse fate than being at Cecilia's school, where they do nothing but be top in exams and have crushes on the teachers and swap library books called *The Madcap of St Monica's*, and such ghastly titles.

Meanwhile a lot of horsy conversation was going on all round us, and snatches of it came drifting to my ears. I wished I could have shunted off Cecilia and joined in. I caught such interesting phrases as 'he didn't look as if he had ever jumped anything higher than two foot six in his life' . . . 'the judge

ordered him straight off the field and that was the end
of him' . . . 'not enough room to do the bending race
at the gallop' . . . 'oh, but she always takes a groom
with her everywhere, so no wonder – ' . . . ' – got
eighteen faults, no I'm not making it up – ' . . .
'believe it or believe it not, those Bartram kids still
ride with the backward seat' . . . 'I'll be back in time
for the first meet of the season, that's the main thing.'

Ann was in a group of people talking about pony
clubs and I could hear them discussing the possibility
of getting up some inter-pony club contests. I heard
somebody else say that their hunting prospects were
dim as their new Master of Foxhounds didn't care
for children and didn't encourage them to follow
on their ponies, much less on bicycles or on foot,
and somebody else said, what a frightful shame,
but perhaps he'd resign or die soon and they'd get
somebody more human.

Then Clarissa Dandleby started talking, and when
her foghorn voice was uplifted nobody else's stood
a chance. She said her father was going to take her
to Ireland for the bloodstock sales. She said that
she couldn't understand people who didn't attend
bloodstock sales as it was always possible to pick
up a bargain cheap. Somebody else said, what did
she mean by cheap? and she said, for instance, her
father had picked up a marvellous pony for only
three thousand pounds, and everybody looked blank
and said Oh.

My cousin Cecilia said, 'I used to like Clarissa
when she went to my school but now I think she's
quite mad,' and I said I couldn't agree more.

Mrs Whirtley then gave us A Look, and said, 'Tea

is over, you know, and we have such a lot of work still to do.'

The work was mostly about who should run the sideshows, such as selling ice cream and helping on the Bring and Buy stall. Nobody was very keen to do these sordid tasks, but Ann and I offered to do an hour on the cake raffle as long as it didn't interfere with any of the classes we were entering for in the gymkhana. Nobody wanted to do anything after tea except watch the open jumping, until Cecilia said in a shattering way that she didn't give a hoot for the open jumping, and as the handicrafts exhibition and the decorated dinner tables competition would be completely organised by then she would be glad to do anything that Mrs Whirtley wanted. Everybody stared dumbly at Cecilia, partly in horror at the ghastly sight of somebody who didn't want to watch open jumping, and partly in the realisation that un-horsy people might even have their uses.

Then the meeting was over, and the taxi came for me and Cecilia. Ann said, 'Good luck,' and with a sinking heart I watched her ride off on George, leading Black Boy who gave me a hurt sort of look.

'To think I'm going to stay at your darling little cottage again,' said Cecilia, 'and sleep in that sweet little bedroom with the sloping roof.' She wasn't being sarky, she really meant it, but my heart slithered down another foot or so as I realised that Cecilia would be having my room, and I would have to go on the divan in the apple room, and she would probably make rude remarks about my pony frieze, but when we got home and she saw it she merely said, 'Well, it's a change from Mickey Mouse.'

I didn't rise to this, as by now I was used to Cecilia trying to make me feel about six.

10 A novice hack

After Cecilia had unpacked and had told Mummy how much she adored her last book, *Angeline, the Fairy Child*, and asked if she was writing another – which is the way you talk to authors – I began to fidget about and Mummy said, what was the matter with me, and couldn't I think of any way to entertain Cecilia, good gracious she was my only cousin and I didn't see her often.

Cecilia said, 'I expect Jill's dying to go and have a riding lesson or something?' and I said, 'You never said a truer word. I'm supposed to go and get some coaching from Mrs Darcy for the novice hack class.'

Cecilia said she would just as soon read, so very relieved I tore off to get my bike and disappear before she could get the bright idea of coming with me.

Mrs Darcy was ready for me, with Sandy Two. I mounted him and of course fifteen hands felt tall to me. It wasn't as if I was like Wendy Mead, used to a stable where you had to ride anything. I trotted Sandy Two round the paddock. He was very well-schooled and answered my rather nervous aids, until he suddenly realised that I was not in complete control and began to snatch at the reins.

'Ride him, Jill!' Mrs Darcy yelled in her impatient

way. 'Keep him balanced. You've got your weight on your forehand.'

I brought Sandy Two back and managed a smooth halt.

'I wish you'd tell me exactly what I'll have to do on the day,' I said. 'I've been reading my equitation books and they say "the judges will expect you to do this-and-that-and-the-other". It's baffling.'

'The judges won't require you to do anything you're not perfectly capable of doing already,' said Mrs Darcy. 'You only need to use your common sense. Now come on, Sandy, show Jill what you can do.'

She mounted Sandy Two herself and demonstrated a collected walk, while I looked on. She halted, turned on the forehand, reined back and circled. Then she made me walk beside her and told me to notice how Sandy Two was using his hocks, and to see that he always did, and to use my legs to keep him up to the bridle.

'He goes well with you,' I said with a sigh like a furnace bellows. 'If only I could make him do the same for me.'

'Don't talk like an idiot,' she said sharply. 'You've been reading too many books. An ounce of practice is worth a ton of theory, even in – or especially in – equitation. Now let's have a show. I'll be the judge and you do your stuff.'

I mounted, and said rather feebly, 'Shall I start by entering the ring?'

'Well, where else would you enter,' said Mrs Darcy. 'The tea tent?'

I entered an imaginary ring and rode Sandy Two

round at a walk, trot, and canter. He went very well, and I was rather thrilled when Mrs Darcy as the judge called me in to stand in an imaginary first place.

'Now will you do a show, please,' she said. 'Anything you like.'

I wanted to giggle, because I couldn't think what to do, but I thought wildly of a book I had read the previous night, something about cantering on each leg in turn. So I tried that, and it partly came off and was partly a bit messy. The worst of it was I couldn't think what else to do, and just went cantering on.

'Could you possibly walk in and rein back?' said Mrs Darcy impatiently.

I thought I managed that rather well, and I dismounted and took the saddle off, and got Sandy Two's legs arranged, and waited for the 'judge' to look him over.

'We'll cut that,' said Mrs Darcy. 'Now lead him out in hand at a trot, and try and look a bit dignified yourself. There's no need to gallop alongside with your hat slipping.'

I tried to look dignified, which wasn't easy as Sandy Two seemed to be enjoying this bit and wasn't anxious to turn. I had a job to push him round, and we got back to the 'judge' with my hat straight but my collar up at one side. I pulled it round and settled my tie.

'It would look better,' Mrs Darcy said, 'if you could manage not to need to dress yourself until you get out of the ring. That'll do. You can stay on and practise a bit.'

'What place are you giving me?' I asked.

'Oh, I'd probably give you Reserve if the others weren't very good.'

I felt squashed, and said that I didn't think the competition would be all that hot in the novice hack class at Mrs Whirtley's fête, and Mrs Darcy squashed me still lower by observing that even if there was practically no competition at all, no real rider would think of aiming at anything less than perfection.

I stayed on and practised for another half-hour. Sandy Two was a lovely hack and made for showing, and I knew I was very lucky indeed to have such a chance, and that if we didn't do well it would be my fault and mine alone.

Wendy Mead came out and watched me. I asked her rather feebly what she thought my chances were on the day, and she said in a sinister voice, 'You'd better be first!'

This made me feel like the heroine in a thriller when she hears the mystery warning over the telephone, but I wasn't going to let Wendy see I was rattled, so I cantered up to her, did a beautiful halt, slid down, and said 'He's a lovely horse and he has a lovely long stride.'

'It'll be lovelier and longer when you get your knees to him properly,' was all that Wendy said, but as we walked in she said, 'By the way, did you give that Dean child your old riding clothes?'

'Why?' I said.

'Because she wears them all over the place, and it looks so silly. She told somebody you had given them to her. You'd have done better to give her a cotton frock.'

'She likes wearing them,' I said, wondering why on earth I was sticking up for Dinah Dean. 'I expect it helps her to pretend she's got a pony.'

'What a crazy idea!' said Wendy.

It was late, so I helped to rub Sandy Two down, and then I jumped on my bike and whizzed home pretty fast – as the brakes don't work anyway – and did a dirt-track swerve round the cottage to the back door.

Mummy and Cecilia were having cocoa and buns in the sitting-room.

'Gosh, I'm hungry!' I said.

'And how many poor ponies have collapsed under you tonight?' said Cecilia pleasantly.

'Sixteen,' I said. 'Seventeen if you count the donkey.'

Mummy told her that I was practising to ride one of Mrs Darcy's horses in a competition, and that flattened her down a bit, especially as Mummy laid it on about how good I was, which was flattering and kind of Mummy, if untrue.

11 A china pony

The next day Mummy said that she would take Cecilia and me to Rychester for a treat, and we would do the shops and have lunch and perhaps go to a cinema. I wanted to go, because there was a shop in Rychester where they sold little china models of horses and I wanted to gaze at these and see how much they were and wonder if I could afford one.

We went the twenty miles on the bus and it took an hour. My one idea was to get to the china shop, but before long I came to the conclusion that it is a mistake to go shopping with unsympathetic people. Now if I had been shopping with Ann or Diana Bush we should have made a beeline for that particular shop with the horses, but Mummy and Cecilia had vastly different ideas and I daren't tell them what I wanted without provoking some of Cecilia's most sarky remarks, while even Mummy would be apt to say, 'Must we have horses all the time, even in Rychester?'

The minute we arrived there Cecilia said she wanted to go and see the cathedral. I could see this appealed to Mummy, as she is very keen on architecture and ancient stones of a mouldering nature, and she knows an awful lot about the cathedral and loves to show people round it, so

I smothered my feelings and we walked round all the medieval tombs and admired the windows, and Cecilia went on about Gothic and Perpendicular until I was nearly choking. I kept thinking they had had enough, and then they would come across a case full of ancient documents and off they would go again.

When it was twenty past eleven, I said, couldn't we go and have an ice? Mummy said, 'But we've only just had breakfast. Good gracious, it simply can't be twenty past eleven!' and Cecilia said how funny it was that you never noticed the time when you were enjoying yourself.

We went to a café opposite the cathedral called *The Buzzing Beehive* and I had a rather soapy ice and Mummy and Cecilia had coffee. I ate my ice in about four seconds, but they were ages over their coffee. I said, weren't we going to the shops? and Mummy said, yes of course, she wanted to get some curtain lining at Smith's, and Cecilia said, was there a very good wool shop nearby? Mummy said that Smith's had a frightfully good wool department. I could see them in Smith's for hours choosing curtain stuff and knitting wool!

I said, could I go and do some shopping by myself? Mummy said in a dim and tactless way, 'What is it you want to buy?'

I said I just wanted to look at some shops, and Mummy said I'd better go to Smith's with them as while they were there it would be a chance to look at some school shirts for me for next term.

The rest of the morning passed drearily by, and soon it was one o'clock and we were all feeling hungry. We went to a café called *The Wagging*

Windmill for lunch, and had hors-d'oeuvre and rolls
and fruit salad.

Cecilia said that if we were going to the cinema in
the afternoon, could we go to the one where there
was that film about African natives cultivating the
jungle, called *Kibwa*?

I wanted to say Help! but I just said, 'I've seen
it.'

Mummy said, 'Where?'

I said, 'At school last term. Some relation of
Miss Grange-Dudley's came and gave a running
commentary on it. It was ghastly.'

Cecilia said, 'You can't have seen it. It's absolutely new. It was only generally released about a
week ago.'

I said, 'Well, I've seen it and that's that,' and she
said again, 'You can't have,' and Mummy said, 'I
don't think you can have seen it, Jill, it must have
been something like it,' and I said, 'I know it was
Kibwa because the relation of Miss Grange-Dudley
was the man who took the film in Africa, and it was
so deadly boring we all went to sleep.'

Mummy ended this argument by asking if there
wasn't anything else we'd like to go to, and I said
the only decent film ever made was *My Friend Flicka*
and I wouldn't mind seeing it ten times.

Cecilia said I couldn't expect them to have a film
about horses in every single cinema in Rychester just
for my benefit, and I said, 'OK, you go and see that
jungle stuff, and I'll go shopping.'

We were now back where we started, because
Mummy promptly said, 'What do you want to go
shopping for, Jill?' and I mumbled, 'Oh, nothing.'

In the end we went to a Walt Disney film, and it was very good, only I couldn't think of anything but those little china horses and how I was being frustrated at every turn by the Hand of Fate, like people in books.

When we came out of the cinema it was a quarter to five, and Cecilia said she would treat us to tea before we went to catch our bus at five thirty. I thought, I shan't be in Rychester again for ages, because Mummy doesn't like me to go there alone, and it has got to be like this!

Mummy led the way towards a café called *The Deadly Daffodil*, or some such sordid name, and I felt it was now or never, so I said I definitely didn't want any tea, and while they were having theirs could I possibly go to Pitt's the tailors about having my black coat let out, and then meet them at the bus?

To my joy Mummy said, 'Yes, you can if you want to, but you've only had that coat a year. You'll have to eat less,' and Cecilia said, 'All these hard-riding women have figures like feather-beds.'

I fled before Mummy could change her mind, and of course I had to go to Pitt's before I went to the china shop, and there wasn't much time. In Pitt's I had to wait while an ancient character with a droopy moustache dithered on about whether he wanted large checks or small checks on his new coat. It was ghastly waiting. He couldn't make up his mind, then he asked Mr Pitt which he would suggest, and Mr Pitt said the small checks were smarter, and the Trying Customer said he preferred the large ones, and so it went on, and after about another ten minutes he said he would think it over and come in again tomorrow.

My business didn't take long, as Mr Pitt said he would make time to do my coat any time I could spare it, and I said I would send it by post, and then I was galloping along High Street and looking for the turning that went down to the lovely china shop.

The horses were there and they were six pounds each. I decided to buy one out of the ten pound prize money that I had won in the Potato Race. It was thrilling to stand looking at them in the window and decide which one I would have. They were beautiful models, in six different positions, and the colours were very natural. The two I liked best were a bay hunter in the act of cropping grass – he had such lovely long legs – and a sturdier chestnut pony with an arched neck and a black mane tossed by the wind. It was awful trying to choose, because it was ten past five already and I couldn't linger, so I decided on the chestnut pony because he had a look of my own Black Boy.

I went in and bought him, and when I was getting out the money I saw a white china basket to hold about two roses and thought it would be nice for Mummy's room, if not too expensive. It turned out to be three pounds fifty, so I bought that too, and the assistant put both things into a parcel and I went charging off to the bus station.

My watch must have been slow because there to my horror was the Chatton bus, just starting up, and I saw the frenzied face of Mummy at the window with her mouth going, Hurry up!

I tore across the square and grabbed the bus handrail and jumped for the platform. The conductor grabbed me and pulled me on, and crash! down went my parcel at his feet. It was an awful crunchy crash of broken china.

Nearly choking with despair I said, 'It doesn't matter,' as he kindly picked up the sagging parcel and handed it to me. I shoved it just as it was into my coat pocket. I had gone through so much to get it, and now this!

Mummy hadn't noticed the crash. She said, 'This is ridiculous, Jill, I'm very annoyed with you. You know what time the bus leaves, must you always be late?'

I said I was sorry, and then sat wretchedly looking out at the ugly houses and dismal fields that slipped by the windows in endless succession. It was evidently my unlucky day and Fate didn't intend me to have one of those lovely horses.

As soon as we got home I rushed out to do the ponies' feeds. In the privacy of the shed while I measured out oats, I thought I could not bear to see the chestnut pony in bits and I would throw the parcel away just as it was, but then I thought perhaps I could do something with glue, though from the crunchiness of the parcel I hadn't much hope.

So I opened it. Mummy's china basket was smashed into a hundred pieces, and my little horse had hardly so much as a chip! He must have been on top of the basket and the basket took all the blow.

I was so excited I hugged him, and decided to call him Invictus, which in case you don't know means Unconquered.

But at the same time I felt that Mummy had been done out of her present, so I planned to go into

Chatton when I had some more pocket money and buy her something that would do instead.

I wrapped Invictus in a lot of paper and put him on the shelf behind the hens' meal bin. I couldn't put him in my room because Cecilia was there.

12   Fun on the common

The next morning Mummy said, 'What are you two girls going to do today?'

I said that Ann was coming round and we were going for a ride, and would probably meet Diana Bush and her brother James who were back from London. Cecilia said that in that case she would sit in the orchard and embroider something for the handicrafts exhibition.

Mummy said, 'Nonsense, you must go with the others, on Jill's bike, and have a ride on Rapide when you get to the Common.'

Cecilia (who in spite of all that she said about horsy people rather fancied herself as a rider, and held the weird theory that nobody needed lessons and all one had to do was to hang on to the pony and urge it to dash madly about) was taken with this idea, but said she hadn't any clothes. So Mummy produced her own very nice brown trousers and a matching silk shirt, and Cecilia put them on. They made her look very sophisticated, and she walked about in front of the long glass in Mummy's room until I felt sick.

I said cheekily, 'Come on, Horrible. Ann's been waiting for ages.'

Ann had George, I took Rapide, and Cecilia rode the bike. When we came to the steep hill we dismounted and led the ponies up, but Cecilia stood on her pedals and rode up to the top, where she waited for us in a very showing-off way.

'Do you walk up all the hills?' she said. 'You'll make the ponies soft.'

We said that we weren't anxious to start a morning's riding with blown and sweaty ponies, and Cecilia said that horses in good condition were never blown and sweaty, but of course riding grass-fed ponies we wouldn't know.

Ann said to me, 'Does she know anything about riding?' and I said, 'No, she makes it up as she goes on.'

When we got to the Common we met Diana and James, and strangely enough Cecilia took to them at once. Just as everything that Ann and I did was wrong, everything that Diana and James did was right. Diana was slim and tall and was riding a very graceful pony called Sylvia, and James who was seventeen was on a spirited cob which really belonged to his father.

I don't know if you have noticed how a boy always shows off when he is with girls. James showed off disgustingly. He did a circus trick of vaulting on to the cob, and then gave a rocky exhibition of the gallop with crossed stirrups and folded arms. Diana said, 'He is a fool, Daddy has told him not to do that,' but Cecilia was impressed.

James jumped a ditch and made a perfect landing, more by good luck than anything else, as I saw him clutch the cob's mane and nearly lose his seat, but Cecilia clapped and said, 'I say, you are most frightfully good!'

'Oh, I'm not so hot really,' said James looking conceited.

'If you ask me, James,' said Diana in a sisterly way, 'you did a rotten jump there. You always do take off too soon.'

James wouldn't have that, and they argued. At last Diana said, 'Well, let's have a competition. Canter to the funny tree with the lump on it, turn, and back on the other leg, and we'll do the timing with the stop watch. Who'll go first?'

'You,' said Ann. 'You made it up.'

Diana had chosen a competition that was just Sylvia's cup of tea, she had done it so often. She gave a perfect performance, but James who was timing said she was slow.

Ann went next, but George wasn't happy and didn't change legs at all, so though she beat Diana's time by eleven seconds Ann was disqualified.

Then it was my turn, but when we got to the tree Rapide didn't want to turn, in fact he carried me for twenty yards before I got him round, so I lost a lot of time.

James went last, and did the whole thing perfectly, and in the shortest time. He then asked Cecilia if she wouldn't like to have a try on the cob? Cecilia calmly said she'd love to. I went cold, and said, 'You'd better borrow George from Ann. He's the quietest pony.'

'Good gracious! Anybody would think I was forty and ready for a wheel-chair,' said Cecilia. 'And I don't want a pony who can't do the course properly.'

Ann went red, and began, 'It was my fault that George didn't change legs – ' but Cecilia was already mounting Marquis, or rather was being heaved up kindly by James. I shut my eyes and thought, Help!

Before Cecilia could get her second stirrup Marquis was off. He shot away, and finding himself completely uncontrolled broke into a gallop. I had visions of Cecilia either going right on into the next county and finishing up at the ocean, or else taking a most frightful toss, but actually Marquis was a sensible old hand at competitions, and when he got to the tree he turned and came back, looking like a steeplechaser. How Cecilia hung on I don't know. She certainly wasn't in the saddle when she got back, she was on the cob's neck with her arms round his neck and more or less gripping his hogged mane with her teeth.

She slithered off, sat down smack on the ground, and announced, 'I beat you all for time.'

'You're telling us!' said Ann, and Diana said, 'What you did can hardly be described as a canter.'

Cecilia got up and said she thought cantering was silly anyway, and only for riding schools, and she liked a pony to *go*, and Marquis was the best ride she had ever had.

'You're jolly lucky to be alive,' I said, and she said, 'Some people wouldn't know how to ride anything but a slug. Well, it's agreed that I won that competition. What shall we do next?'

'There's a lot of brushwood about,' said Ann. 'Let's strip some poles and stick them up and have a bending race.'

'Isn't that a bit kiddish?' said Cecilia.

'It's jolly good exercise for control,' said James.

We all began to collect long pieces of brushwood

and strip them and stick them up in two rows. This had necessarily to be done in rather soft ground, which would slow the race down and make us careful.

'Jill and Ann can ride off first,' said Diana. 'Then James and I, then the two winners, and Cecilia can ride with the finalist.'

Ann's George and my Rapide were old hands at bending. Neither of them got the speed they might have done, but they started well, turned at the end without losing ground, and zigzagged back beautifully. We finished neck and neck, and had to do it again. This time George's forward leap carried him ahead and he got into a gallop before Rapide, but paid for his extra speed by overshooting the turning-post, and I got home by a length.

Then Diana and James got away. James was apt to whack the cob round, which Marquis didn't like. He was really too spirited for a bending race and while he pranced Diana won by two lengths.

Then it was Diana's turn to ride it off with me. I had met her many a time in the show ring at this competition, and she usually beat me. I took it for granted that she would do so today, because Rapide wasn't at his best on the softish ground. I saw as we came up towards the finish that Diana was nearly a length ahead, but James shouted, 'You missed a pole!'

'I jolly well didn't,' I said.

'Not you, you dope. Diana. You've won, Jill.'

Diana panted, slapped her chest, and said, 'Well, it's you and Cecilia now, Jill. Which horse do you want, Cecilia?'

I was certain she would choose Marquis again and probably break her neck, and after all I was responsible for her, but to my relief she said she would have Sylvia, as she was sure Sylvia would have won the last heat easily if she hadn't missed the pole.

She lumbered up on to Sylvia and fussed over the stirrups. Sylvia looked bored with this, and when James shouted Go! She made a bad start. Cecilia kicked like mad and yelled, 'Get on, you! Gallop, can't you!' Needless to say this did not impress Sylvia who was used to aids, not shouting, and she was only turning the bottom pole when I finished.

'If I'd taken Marquis I'd have won,' said Cecilia, and we didn't bother to argue about this, though James said, 'You shouldn't neck-rein like a polo-player, you should use your legs.'

To my surprise Cecilia accepted this criticism meekly, and even said she supposed speed wasn't everything. This was amazing coming from Cecilia who had previously recognised no other pace than a gallop. I began to have hopes of her.

James said, 'Now let's each do a show, five minutes of anything you like, and Cecilia can judge who gets the Gold Challenge Cup and the Imperial Certificate of Magnificent Equitation.'

Cecilia looked pleased. James said that as he was already on Marquis he would go first. We all knew that this kind of thing was just up his street, as while he was staying in London he had done some practising in a covered school with a dressage coach.

James did everything he knew, and it looked terrific to see him making delicate intricate movements in the bright sunshine with the green Common all round, and even if he was more showy than accurate we would all have liked to be able to do as well. Then Diana had her turn, and of course she had learned a lot from practising with James, and Sylvia being rather a vain pony there was quite a lot of tail-flicking and neck-arching mixed up with the dressage.

Then I gave Rapide a chance to show what all his recent schooling had done for him, and he behaved beautifully and I only wished we could have been in a real show ring, and finally Ann did some perfect figures of eight on George.

Cecilia said that everybody was good, but actually she had liked Diana's show best, so we made Diana come up to receive the Challenge Cup – which was a spray of blackberry flowers – and bow to the judge, and she pretended to drop the cup on his toe and we all yelled.

The main point was that from that moment Cecilia realised that there was more in riding than clutching on to a pony and dashing about, and I never heard another sarky word from her, in fact when a bit later I asked her if she would like a ride on Rapide while I rode the bike she asked me if she was sitting properly, and how to do a collected walk, which was nearly unbelievable to anyone who had previously known my dear cousin.

We had a wonderful morning and as usual got home late for lunch and were flayed alive by Mummy, whose Thing is a morbid passion for being punctual at meals.

In the afternoon I found that Rapide had a loose shoe so I took him to the farrier's. I told Mr

Ramsbuckle about the fête and made him promise to come and bring the whole of the local farriers' union, or whatever they call themselves.

Just then Wendy Mead rode up on one of her father's farm horses, with tack that needed repairing slung round her shoulders.

While we waited she said, 'Your friend Dinah Dean has done it now!'

I went cold, and said, 'She isn't my friend, and I wish I'd never given her the clothes, and what's she done anyway?'

'She's been riding a pony in the middle of the night – quite a lot of nights, I gather. It's in a field at Watson's farm, in fact it's Mary Watson's pony. Mary had an idea several nights ago that something queer was happening. Then she looked out of her bedroom window about midnight and thought she saw somebody riding the pony in the field, but it wasn't a clear night and in the morning she thought she must have dreamed it. However, the next night the moon was up, and Mary distinctly saw somebody riding her pony. She told her father, and the next night Mr Watson lay in wait and caught Dinah at it.'

'What did he do?'

'He couldn't do much,' said Wendy heatedly, 'but he gave Dinah a fright and sent her packing, and Mary says if it happens again Dinah will be jolly sorry.'

'And I suppose you're going to tell me that she was wearing my clothes?' I said, and Wendy said, 'I wouldn't know, but it looks to me as if you've started something. That kid's a menace.'

I didn't say anything, but I knew the whole village would be talking about the Watson affair, and I wished I could get hold of Dinah and find out what she was up to, and stop her.

The next day Cecilia went home. In the morning she went down to Chatton on my bike and bought presents for Mummy and me. She bought Mummy a painted tile to stand a teapot on, and she bought me a book about arranging flowers. I thought it was very kind of her, and Mummy was reading my book for days after and saying what good ideas it had, like having sprays of carrot tops in an old saucepan with a few gladioli mixed in, and everybody was happy so that was all right.

13 A pony for sale

The more I thought of it, the more I felt I had got to see Dinah Dean. It wasn't easy to find time, as in the holidays I usually arrange with my friends to spend all the days doing something with the ponies, and also I get let in for the usual domestic chores, as doubtless you do too. However, there came a wettish afternoon, and Ann had a cold and her fussy mother wouldn't let her ride, so I put on a mac and found myself whizzing off to Dinah's house.

Dinah opened the door. When she saw me she went red and looked as if she was going to cry. She said, 'Will you come in? I'm just doing some cooking.'

We went into a horrid dark kitchen, and Dinah took a rather messy cake out of the oven and started scraping the burnt bits off.

I said, 'What on earth have you been doing? You'll get into prison, and everybody will know they're my clothes.'

She said, 'Well, I had simply got to learn to ride, and I can now, and it didn't do the pony any harm.'

'You can't call that riding,' I pointed out.

'Yes, you can,' she said. 'I watched people, and I got a book out of the library and copied nearly all of it out and learnt it off by heart.'

'But you didn't have any tack, did you?' I said.

'No, I learnt bareback which made it harder, but I sat properly and did everything as it said, and the pony liked me and she was marvellous.'

I told her that Mary Watson was going to murder her, and so would I if anybody did that with one of my ponies. She just looked at me, and said, 'Could I possibly have a ride on your pony some day?'

'Gosh!' I said. 'What frightful cheek!'

'I wouldn't do him any harm,' she said, 'and I'd pay for it by cleaning out hens or anything you like.'

'You don't want much!' I said. 'Mary Watson would think I was backing you up and she'd murder me too.'

'I suppose it wouldn't do,' said Dinah, looking miserably at the horrid cake. 'But the only thing I want to do in the world is ride and I do adore ponies so.'

'Wouldn't your father pay for some lessons for you?' I said.

She shook her head and said, 'Whenever I ask him he always says, "Don't bother me, can't you see I'm busy?" He's always doing figures and making charts and things, and he never really notices anything in ordinary life. I take him his supper and he reads papers all the time he's eating it, and then about an hour after he says, "Aren't we going to have any supper tonight?"'

'Well, I'll have to go,' I said, 'but honestly, Dinah, you'll have to stop doing awful things, especially in my clothes.'

She started to cry and said, 'I wish I'd never had them, you can take them back if you want.'

I felt sorry for her, because having been poor and proud myself once I knew what it felt like. I suddenly wanted to say that she could come round one evening and have a ride on Black Boy, but I thought the whole village would hear about it and think I was backing Dinah.

The next day I told Ann all about it, and she said she thought I was really mean and ought to have offered her a ride, as whatever the village thought it was the duty of a true sportsman to encourage the young entry, and I said you couldn't really call Dinah the young entry as she was more of a gate-crasher.

However you know how awkward one's Better Feelings are when they get hold of one, one just can't do anything about it, so I went back to Dinah's. When she opened the door I blurted out, 'You can have a ride on Black Boy.'

She lit up like a Christmas tree, and said, 'Oh. How gorgeous! When?'

I said, 'I don't want anybody to see, so we'll have to be a bit conspirator-ish. You know that crossroads on the Common with a broken-down cottage on one side and the beginning of the woods on the other?'

She said she did, and I went on, 'Meet me there in about an hour and I'll bring the ponies. We can ride in the woods where nobody will see us.'

I dashed off and got the ponies, and felt a bit like Guy Fawkes starting out to blow up the Houses of Parliament, and when I got to the aforesaid crossroads it was all quiet and deserted, and there was Dinah, waiting. I got her up on Black Boy, and I must say she sat very well and knew what to do. I never knew a kid improve her riding so

much under what are known as Adverse Circum-
stances.

We set off into the woods. She kept saying how
marvellous it was, and she did look happy. I led the
way on Rapide.

She said, 'This is something I've dreamed about,
cantering down a forest ride into the romantic depths
of the mighty wood.'

I said, 'Well, as a matter of fact these woods are
very deep and people never come here. I know a
way that nobody on earth knows, I discovered it by
accident when I was a kid, and I'll show you.'

I hadn't thought about it for years, but there was
a secret way I had never told to anybody, not even
my own friends. You broke through what looked
like a dead end of hazel brush, and there a grassy
ride opened out before you and you could go on
winding about among trees for a mile or so till you
came to a sort of fairy clearing in the heart of the
woods.

I took Dinah, and she was very excited. When
she saw the little clearing she said, 'Wouldn't it be
wonderful to live here for ever? Nobody would be
able to find you, and there's grass for the pony and
you could eat nuts and blackberries.'

I said, yes, it would be rather gorgeous, but I didn't
see myself having the chance to do it, and we'd better
be turning home.

When we got back to civilisation again she started
thanking me for the ride till she was nearly blue in
the face, and I was glad I had done it for her. I said
perhaps someday when I had time I'd let her have
another ride, only she'd have to jolly well behave

herself meanwhile, and she looked rather thoughtful and opened her mouth to say something and then shut it again, and I said, 'What's the matter?' and she said, 'Nothing,' then she said, 'Thanks a million,' and went dashing off.

I went round to Ann's to tell her I'd given Dinah a ride and that the Good Deed was over, thank goodness, but when I got to the Derrys' house it was only to find a scene of wild drama, as Ann's little sister Pam had been riding Ann's old pony Seraphine and had been bucked off at a jump and was in bed with concussion.

Mrs Derry was so fussy she behaved as if she wasn't quite all there, and proved to be the most hopeless kind of mother for any horsy person to have, as one minute she was saying that Pam must never ride again, and the next minute that Ann must never ride again, and that she would sell Seraphine. Ann looked furious, and I pointed out to Mrs Derry that every single rider who ever lived took tosses and that Pam would probably have dozens before she died – as I had had myself in my long experience as a rider – and the whole point was that Pam had never learned to fall properly, but she would in time.

Unfortunately this only made Mrs Derry worse, and after breathing out a lot of dire threats she said that Seraphine was dangerous and would definitely have to go.

At this Ann began to cry, as she was fond of Seraphine who had once been her pony when she was smaller, but she had to admit that Seraphine's temper had been a bit uncertain lately and if she didn't want to jump she was apt to buck. That, however, was no reason for selling her, as one would not sell one's aged aunt for similar reasons.

Pam was all right in a day or two, and Ann told her she would slay her if she didn't say it was entirely her own fault that Seraphine threw her. Pam did say it, but it was no good, Mrs Derry was adamant. She began to draft an advertisement for the *Rychester Weekly*, a worthy but stodgy paper which is read all over the county by persons who want to buy houses and antique furniture and to sell things like sewing machines and – unfortunately – ponies.

Ann and I had hoped that we might be allowed to draft the advertisement, as we had planned to make it so unattractive that nobody would want to buy Seraphine, but we were not allowed. The morning after the advertisement appeared Ann had visions of the postman staggering under a load of offers for Seraphine, but such was not the case. There was not a single letter and our spirits rocketed up. The next afternoon Mrs Derry went out in the car, and I went to tea with Ann. While we were sitting in the dining-room arguing about something or other, the doorbell rang.

We looked at each other in a bleak sort of way and said, Seraphine! Then we rushed to the front door. A farming character stood there, and I instantly took a dislike to him. He had funny little eyes and the kind of hair which looks like a badly thatched cottage, and I have noticed that persons with hair like this are not fond of animals.

He said, 'Name of Derry? My name's Mr Towtle. I read in the *Weekly* that you've got a pony for sale. Like to have a look at it, if it's cheap.'

Ann went red and said, 'It isn't cheap.'

I said quickly, 'It isn't for sale, it's all a mistake,' and shut the door before Mr Towtle, left outside, could think what to say next. We peeped through the glass, and after scratching his head a few times he went away.

'Gosh, Jill, you were marvellous,' said Ann, and I said, 'That's the only way to do it, and we've got to get rid of everybody who comes the same way.' Ann said that her mother wouldn't be out every afternoon, and she couldn't be sitting all the time waiting to get to the front door first, so we made a lot of plans to keep Mrs Derry out of the way, like getting Mummy and Diana Bush's mother and a few others to invite her out to tea every day, but actually we hadn't much hope.

Nobody else called that afternoon, and Mrs Derry came home and fortunately didn't ask if anyone had called about the pony. I went home, and Ann told me next morning that she had lain awake most of the night dreading what the postman might bring in the chilly dawn. However, in the chilly dawn she fell fast asleep, and didn't wake till nine o'clock and got into a row for being late for breakfast. There were several opened letters by Mrs Derry's plate, and Ann managed to get a squint at them and saw to her relief that they were only bills and effusions from distant relations, which was comforting.

We began to hope again, and to cheer ourselves up by remembering that the end of the summer wasn't a good time for selling ponies, and so on.

Then the blow fell. A woman in a camel coat arrived one afternoon with a boy of about ten and

Mrs Derry opened the door herself, and we heard the woman say, 'I believe you have a pony for sale.'

Ann pushed her fingers in her ears, which I thought was a feeble thing to do as one might as well know The Worst. The next thing, we saw Mrs Derry taking the woman and the boy down to see Seraphine, and I had a feeling that All Was Lost.

'I think she looks rather nice,' I said, trying to look on the bright side like the awful children in Mummy's books.

'The boy looked fairly OK, too,' said Ann miserably. We both sat biting our nails, picturing the sordid scene that must by now be taking place in Seraphine's loosebox.

About twenty minutes later Pam burst in and said that Seraphine was sold. The woman's name was Mrs Arden and the boy's name was William, and he was having riding lessons and his father had promised him a pony for his birthday. He was very taken with Seraphine and had always wanted a grey, and had told his mother he wouldn't look at any more ponies because that was the one he wanted, and he was going to work hard at his riding and win a lot of prizes next summer.

When Pam stopped for breath Ann said, 'I think you're beastly hard-hearted, Pam, to sound so bucked about it,' and Pam said she thought Ann was feeble to make such a fuss, and Ann picked up the nearest thing and threw it at Pam and it happened to be Mrs Derry's mending basket, and socks and darning wool and needles and buttons flew all over the place, and we had to pick them up by crawling all over the floor and jam them back in the basket any old how.

Then Mrs Derry came back and told us the sordid transaction was completed and she was pleased at the price Seraphine had fetched, and Mrs Arden was going to send a horse box tomorrow. Ann said, 'The only thing I care about is that Seraphine should go to a good home,' and Mrs Derry said, 'As if I shouldn't be satisfied about that!' and added that Mrs Arden was fond of dogs and a leading light in the Women's Institute, which hadn't anything to do with the pony really but sounded vaguely comforting, especially as the Women's Institute had recently passed a resolution against sending ponies to slaughterhouses.

So we felt less gloomy, though we took care to be out of the way when Seraphine actually left. I mean, there are some things one cannot stand. I regret to say that beastly little Pam, who must have had a heart like a stone, was very interested in the horse box and even helped the man to shove Seraphine up the ramp. It was only when Seraphine was gone that it dawned on Pam that she hadn't got a pony at all now, and wasn't likely to have one, and when Ann firmly refused ever to let her ride George she cried and yelled, and it served her jolly well right.

14 That dreadful Dinah

I went up to Mrs Darcy's and practised every night on Sandy Two. I was doing much better now, and had gone over the ground a lot of times, but one never has to slacken when schooling a pony or he will get the idea that he can slack on The Day. I worked very hard, though Mrs Darcy was still not satisfied and always seemed to turn up to watch just when I was doing something badly.

She herself had entered for the open jumping at the fête on Blue Smoke, and there were a lot of other entries coming in, including some from friends of Captain Cholly-Sawcutt who would be worth watching. At our next committee meeting at Blossom Hall, Mrs Whirtley was very bucked about this, and when she learned that I knew Captain Cholly-Sawcutt and had sold him tickets she went boiled puce colour with joy, and Clarissa Dandleby's eyes popped out like organ stops, and afterwards two kids actually asked me for my autograph. The tea was as good as ever and everybody was in a good humour and dying for the actual fête to happen and Cecilia had had entries for heaps of handicrafts and decorated dinner-tables so she was happy too, and altogether our Joy was Unconfined as Shakespeare or somebody says.

I rode home thinking that life wasn't too bad at all, but I had hardly got into the house when Mummy came out of the sitting-room and said, 'Oh dear, Jill, that unfortunate Dean child has got into really bad trouble this time.'

I nearly sat down flat on the floor. I just said, 'What?'

'Well, it's rather awful,' said Mummy. 'They say she's stolen some ponies.'

'She's – what?' I gasped.

'She's stolen three ponies from a shed in some farmer's field and she and the ponies have disappeared.'

'How do they know it was her?' I said.

'Because apparently the farmer has had to warn her off his land several times. He was always noticing her hanging about the shed and looking in through the window. And once in the evening he saw her try the door and chased her, but she got away. She's very thin and quick, you know. And as I said, she's disappeared. Her father hasn't seen her since seven o'clock last night. In a way I think it serves him right for not looking after her better, and I think he's learnt his lesson and when he gets Dinah back he'll make her happier at home.'

'Oh,' was all I said, as I walked off to the orchard to think. I just couldn't understand it, and neither could anybody else. Everybody was talking about this strange affair, and thinking that Dinah would soon turn up, but she didn't. She and the three ponies had completely disappeared and it was a first-class mystery in Chatton, as you can imagine. I felt that being more or less mixed up with Dinah's doings, she and I might end our days shut up in some dungeon.

This quite put me off riding, which wasn't a good thing at all with the fête so near at hand. I tried to convince myself that nobody could really blame me, as I had only tried to be encouraging to the young entry in the manner of a true sportsman, and that the best thing I could do was to forget it and concentrate on Sandy Two and the under-fourteen jumping and the other things I had entered for at the gymkhana. However, as you probably know, when you have something on your mind it does jolly well put you off, and I wished I had never set eyes on that beastly little Dinah or done Good Deeds to her.

Ann and I practised competitions together all day long, and every time I did anything badly she said, 'What's gone wrong with you?' and I said, 'Oh, dry up!' and so it went on. There was I with my guilty secret – if you can call it a guilty secret, merely having given Dinah a ride on my pony – but it felt guilty to me, what with the clothes and everything. I honestly rather hoped that she had been whisked away by the fairies and would never appear again, but the fact was that she had run away from home and taken three of somebody else's ponies with her, and everybody was asking where could she be? Also by now the police were looking for her. It was awful.

And then in the middle of the night, which is the time when one's best ideas often come to one, I woke and sat straight up in bed. Gosh! I thought. The fairy glade in the woods, the place I showed her. I wonder!

I had got to get there and see.

It was jolly difficult, as I had planned a busy day for next day. About six of us were going up to Diana's

and James's farm to do jumps and competitions, and
we were going to take sandwich lunches and have a
picnic in their orchard. There were my sandwiches
to make, the ponies to feed and groom, and I
had to be off by nine thirty. What on earth was
I going to do?

All I could do was to get up frightfully early and
be off to the woods about six, before anybody was
around. I set my alarm clock for six, and it worked,
and I jumped clean out of bed on the first buzz, and
it was jolly cold as lovely summer days often are
before they start, if you know what I mean. I put
on my shorts and a wool sweater and tiptoed out. I
was terrified that Mummy would hear me and ask
where I was going, for she would certainly think I
had gone mad, as early rising and skipping about in
the dew are not among my strong points.

But there wasn't a sound from her room. I
slipped out of the back door and went to wake
up Black Boy, who was very surprised indeed.
Soon we were off, and we had the world to ourselves and it was very pretty, as it is at that hour
of the morning if you are brave enough to try
it.

The air smelt good, everything glowed with a
goldy light, a lot of larks were singing madly in
the pinkish sky, and other little birds jibbered and
jabbered happily in the hedges. Not that I was feeling
very birdy. I was wondering what I should do if I
didn't find Dinah where I thought I should find her.
Then I thought, why worry? If she isn't there she's
probably disappeared for ever and ever. I cheered
up and said good morning to some passing farm

workers who didn't look at all surprised to see me riding so early.

I got to the woods and rode on and on into the depths, far beyond where people usually go, and I broke through the hazel thickets and found the secret ride, and went on and on winding among the trees the way I knew until I came to the edge of the clearing and there I stopped.

In the clearing were three horses, two fast asleep and one nosing the fine grass. There was a big percheron, an old pony, and a young wildish-looking pony. Black Boy gave a little whicker when he saw the other horses, but I told him to be quiet and I slid down and tied him.

I found Dinah in a dry cosy spot between the roots of a big beech tree, curled up fast asleep on the beech mast, wrapped in two grey blankets. She looked as happy and peaceful as could be. Beside her was a basket containing half a loaf of bread, a cup, and three apples.

I said, 'Dinah!' She gave a sort of terrified squeak and jumped right up in one bound. When she saw it was me she just said, 'Oh.'

I said, 'Gosh, you are awful!'

She just said calmly, 'I thought you might turn up. But you're quite right, absolutely nobody else in the world can ever find me here.'

I said, 'Goodness! How long do you think you're going to stay here?' and she said as calmly as before, 'For ever, I should think.'

I said very angrily, 'Now look here, Dinah, I'm not standing for this kind of thing. I mean, stealing horses – '

She went into an absolute fury and yelled, 'You beast! I don't steal! I didn't steal them, I rescued them.'

'What on earth are you talking about?' I said. 'Those are the horses you stole from a farmer's shed, aren't they? Everybody's talking about it.'

'So you don't know?' she said. 'Well, I'll tell you. It's that beast, Mr Towtle. He's going round buying up horses and ponies cheap and selling them to be slaughtered and making a lot of money out of it. *Nice* horses, like those! He keeps a crowd of them all jammed together in that horrible shed in his field, and they're terrified and hungry, and he doesn't even feed them. I wish I could have got them all out instead of just three.'

I gaped at her, and said, 'What did you do?'

'I saw what was going on through the window,' she said, 'and I turned out to be a very good detective. The door had a Yale lock. I fetched a ladder from the farm in the middle of the night and broke the window and got in and opened the door from inside. I told you I could only manage three, one to ride and two to lead, so I picked the hungriest, the ones that had been there longest. When the shed is packed full a van comes in the middle of the night and loads them up. The Towtle beast is afraid of what the neighbourhood would say if they knew.'

'Which one did you ride?' I asked, looking at the three horses.

'The percheron,' said Dinah, and I said, 'You would!' I was struck dumb by this amazing kid.

'You'd have done it yourself,' said Dinah calmly, and I said, 'I wouldn't have had the nerve.'

'I wish I could get three more,' she said, 'but he's guarding the shed now, and I've been out each night and the van has been and fetched a load away. He's got to be stopped, the brute. Those poor horses!'

I honestly didn't know what to say or do. It was all too big and daring for me, and I thought, well if Dinah can cope, let her.

I said, what was she going to do next? and she said, 'Nothing for the present. I'll just stay here. We're all quite happy, but I'll tell you what you can do, you can bring me a loaf of bread now and then and a few apples and leave them on this side of the hazel thicket, and I can fetch them.'

I said, 'OK, I'll do that, but honestly you can't stay here for ever and ever,' and she said, '*Can't* I!'

I said feebly, 'They're awfully nice horses,' and she said, 'I know they are, and that old pony's a lovely ride, he's been somebody's pet. It makes your blood boil. Fortunately there's grazing for them here, and a stream.'

I said, 'I'll bring the bread and things, but it's going to be awfully difficult for me to get away, so don't expect to see me when I come. I'm booked up all the time, getting ready for this fête at Mrs Whirtley's.'

She grinned and said, 'Oh, that's all right.' She gave a little chirrup, and all the horses woke up and came to her and nuzzled her shoulders, and she gave them each one of the apples, leaving herself the dry bread for her breakfast. I shuddered when I thought of them being cruelly treated and sent to some horrible horse butcher. I had to take off my hat to Dinah.

So off I went, and rode home feeling more mixed up than ever. I got home and fed my ponies and the hens, and went in for my own breakfast without any remarks being made.

Then I went round to Diana's farm and made an awful mess of all the competitions, and they said they couldn't imagine what had come over me and I would have to do something about myself before The Day. How true!

15   Wonderful, wonderful stables

I thought I had better pull myself together (as aforesaid) and get the worryful Dinah out of my mind, and strangely enough I did, because Black Boy in some peculiar manner got colic and rolled about on his back in a most hysterical way, and I rang up the vet and he didn't come for ages, and it was only a fortnight off the fête, and I was frantic and had Mummy and Mrs Crosby and everybody else running round in circles. However, the vet came and gave Black Boy a draught and got him into his stall, and I sat with him nearly a whole night, watching the hands of my watch go round so that I shouldn't miss giving him his medicine at the right time. Mummy came out at intervals and said I must come in and go to bed, and she thought I was idiotic and all the rest of it, and I said, You little know! Every time I left Black Boy for even a few minutes he seemed worse when I got back, and he rolled his eyes at me so pathetically. However, when the vet came again he said, 'This animal's playing you up,' and surprisingly enough Black Boy was immediately much better and got up on his feet and looked sheepish.

He was fairly seedy for two days, and it was only when he was all right again that I remembered Dinah and the bread and apples. I thought if she had died

of hunger it would be my fault, but she didn't strike
me as the sort of person who would die of anything,
she was extremely resourceful. I asked Mrs Crosby
for a loaf – we always have plenty – and I picked a
whole bag of apples from our orchard where there are
thousands. They didn't look very ripe, but I guessed
Dinah wouldn't be too particular, and I took the lot
and left them on her side of the hazel thicket and sped
back like the wind.

After that I got on with my ordinary life, which
really I hadn't been able to do for quite a long time,
what with Cecilia and Dinah and Black Boy's colic.
The things one could do if one was left alone to do
them! I had planned to do all kinds of things in the
summer holidays and here they were whizzing by
and hardly anything done at all. At the beginning
the eight weeks had felt like a year, and now they
felt like eight minutes.

I got the ponies back on their routine of careful
schooling, and had a few rides in the evenings with
Ann and Diana Bush. Then I reorganised my tack
room for the winter ahead, and cleaned some of the
stuff that had got pushed into corners, and mended
everything that needed it.

Mrs Crosby grumbled and said I used all her cleaning stuff, and she didn't know what had come over
me, and give her sure and steady all the time instead
of here today and gone tomorrow, and I retorted, 'A
rolling stone gathers no moss and likewise a stitch
in time saves nine, and now think of another one
if you can!' and she said if I was her girl she'd
have something to say about that mending basket,
so just to show her, I reorganised all my clothes too

and mended everything and ironed all my shirts and pressed my jodhs, and she said it *would* be just when she was needing the iron herself! You can't please some people.

Then I remembered Dinah again and thought it was about time she had some more food. You can't think what a job I had to get away for half an hour. Everybody all of a sudden seemed to take such an interest in where I was going. I got a loaf out of the bread bin and had to put it back again. Next time I got it out I met Mummy and she said, 'Darling, I told you only to use the broken bread for the animals.' Finally I managed it, and galloped all the way to the woods and dumped the bread and apples where Dinah would be able to find them.

I didn't stop to see if she was alive or if she had acquired any more horses. But on the way back I suddenly thought, Towtle! That was the horrible man who nearly bought Seraphine! Gosh, what an escape!

I then stopped thinking about Dinah's doings because I had loads of other worries, mainly having to revise my ideas about the fête so as to give Rapide the major part of the work, though the vet had said that Black Boy would be quite fit for his classes. I didn't want to take any risks.

A day or two later Mrs Darcy came cantering up the lane on Blue Smoke and stopped at our gate. She called out, 'Nice weather for the fête!'

I was more or less standing on my head, weeding the path under Mummy's orders, so I said something that sounded like OO-er-ah-um.

'I say!' said Mrs Darcy. 'I've got to go over to the

Cholly-Sawcutt place this afternoon. I wondered if you'd care to come. Ask your mother if you can.'

I was so thrilled that I straightened out in one jump and nearly turned a somersault. I asked Mrs Darcy to wait, and rushed into the cottage where Mummy was sitting at her typewriter with a furrowed brow.

'Mrs Darcy wants – ' I began.

Mummy said, 'Oh, darling! I've been wanting to do this bit properly for about an hour, and just when I get the right sentence you've got to come and drive it right out of my head. What is it?'

I told her, and she looked a bit bleak.

'Stables!' she said. 'I suppose this is what they'd call the Higher Horsemanship. Well, don't get any ideas, will you, Jill? Because I've set my heart on your doing a decent secretarial course when you leave school.'

I looked uncomfortable, because the prospect of going to see the Cholly-Sawcutt stables didn't mix with secretarial courses, and the last thing I wanted was to discuss my future. I just said, 'Oh, Mummy, please say I can go. I want to so much.'

She said I could go, and I tore back and told Mrs Darcy. We set off in her car at two o'clock.

I don't know if you have ever been to a big training stable, but it is the sort of place where if you are a horsy person you could wander about in a dream for hours. The long rows of beautifully kept loose boxes, the broad paved yard, the green paddocks and the jumping field simply dazzled me. We drove into the yard. A lot of people looked very busy, and I couldn't drag my eyes away from the beautiful heads of two hunters looking out over their half doors. There was so much to see, my head kept turning from side to side and I wished it was on a swivel and would go right round.

A manager person came out to speak to Mrs Darcy, and I hoped the business was going to take a long time. It would be awful if it was over in five minutes and I never got any further than this. I wanted to go and look into all those loose boxes and peep into the harness rooms, and wander across the paddocks and examine the jumps, and I was madly excited by the glimpse of a man in the distance who seemed to be breaking in a pony. Just then the vet arrived in his car, and was met by a groom in khaki overalls who led him to a small building in the yard. My feet were itching to follow them and see what was going on there.

The manager said, 'Excuse me a minute,' and went away. I said to Mrs Darcy, 'Gosh, there must be a lot going on here!' and she said, 'Plenty of hard work,' and I said, 'Plenty of fun too.'

'Well, they do a bit of everything,' she said. 'The Captain is particularly good with young horses, and his hunters are noted. He usually has one or two beautiful foals.'

'I expect those are his own practice jumps over there,' I said, in a voice of deep awe.

'They're snorters,' said Mrs Darcy. 'But so beautifully made. I've been round them, but I don't suppose anybody but the Captain has ever jumped a clear round in that field.'

The manager came back and after a few words all seemed to be over; then all of a sudden who should walk out of the house but Captain Cholly-Sawcutt himself.

'Goodness!' called Mrs Darcy. 'I thought you were miles away.'

He greeted us cheerily, and said, 'It just happens that I have a free weekend. In fact I've promised to go to this fête on Saturday and do an exhibition round before the open jumping begins. I rang Mrs Whirtley up and told her I'd come.'

I said, 'I hope everybody knows, then millions will be there.'

'Don't worry,' said Mrs Darcy laughing. 'If I know Phyllis Whirtley she'll have spread the news all over the county by now.'

'Have you sold any more tickets?' said the great man to me in a very friendly way.

'Oh, Jill's been working like a beaver,' said Mrs Darcy. 'If the fête isn't a success it won't be her fault. And she's showing Sandy Two for me in the Novice Hack class.'

'Good for you,' said the Captain. 'You'll have a couple of tough judges in Colonel Brown and Tom Beasley, so it won't be a walkover for anybody. For a small affair this fête is going to be a very big affair, if you get my meaning.'

I stood on one leg and scratched my other ankle and said, 'Oh!'

Mrs Darcy smiled and said, 'I notice that Jill can't keep her eyes off that man of yours who is lunging the colt. I think she'd like to know the sort of work you do here.'

The Captain asked me if I took it that seriously, and I could only go boiled puce colour with excitement and stammer out that I took it more seriously than anything else in the world.

He said, 'If you like, I'll find a boy to take you round,' and I said, 'How absolutely wonderful.'

He said, 'Well, we have about two hundred acres here. At present we're schooling some five- and six-year-olds, and getting the hunters ready for next season. We always have young horses on hand, and it's quite a job finding time to school them. Of course my people ride my horses in all local tests and competitions, and go far afield for dressage tests and cross-country events and road and track events. It means long hours of work for them, so needless to say the only people I employ here are those whose whole life is horses. This isn't just a job, it's a whole way of life. I've got three full-time grooms here, and a new girl who's as keen as mustard, and a boy who's come for experience in making and breaking. I'm away such a lot, I have to have people I can trust absolutely to see that everything goes on as I would have it if I were here.'

'Now you know!' said Mrs Darcy. 'This makes my place look like a baby's playground, doesn't it?'

It did, but I couldn't very well agree without appearing rude.

'By the way,' said the Captain, 'what's all this about some girl in your part of the world walking off with three horses and disappearing?'

I went cold, and Mrs Darcy said, 'Oh, it's the local mystery. She's an odd sort of girl, but where she can have got to with three horses is past imagining. I mean, the police are on the look-out on roads for miles round; she must have daubed herself and the horses all over with invisible paint. It's a nine days' wonder.'

'I hope she isn't one of your pupils,' said the Captain.

'Oh, good gracious no, not likely.'

I edged away while they were talking as I didn't want to hear all this, and was only just in time, as the Captain said, 'It's a bit thick, I mean stealing horses – ' and I opened my big mouth and nearly found myself saying out loud, 'She says she didn't steal them, she rescued them,' and only just stopped myself in time. It was a sticky moment.

The Captain called out, 'Harry!' and a boy of about sixteen came out of a door. 'Take this young lady round and show her everything she fancies to see.' I could hardly believe that this was happening to me.

Harry proved to be an awfully good guide. Soon my ambition was realised, as we went round all the loose-boxes and saw the hunters, and went into the neat professional-looking tack rooms, and he also showed me a new foal a week old whom he said was destined to be a great steeplechaser some day.

I said, 'Do you get any riding here?' and he said, 'Oh, yes! The Captain is a wonderful employer and gives everybody a chance of doing some riding and getting all kinds of experience. I wouldn't have come here otherwise. At some stables you don't get any instruction at all, but here – although I'm actually only the lowest form of life on the place – I'm being taught how to prepare a horse for a cross-country event, and I've also been allowed to ride in one or two showing classes. It makes the life so frightfully interesting.'

'It must be marvellous,' I said, 'to do nothing but horses from morning to night all day long.'

He nodded and said, 'All day long is right. Counting the actual work, and the training I get, and taking the horses to shows, I suppose my average working day is about fourteen hours, but I love it and I don't count it in hours. I mean, there simply isn't anything I'd rather be doing.'

'I'd feel like that too,' I said.

He asked me, was I a girl groom at Mrs Darcy's? and I was so flattered at being taken for one that it was an awful come-down to have to admit that I was still at school. Harry said, 'I expect you're dying to leave and get cracking with horses,' and I said in a very dim sort of way that on the contrary I was going to take a secretarial course, and my mother wanted me to go to a family in Switzerland to get French and German. Harry just said, Oh.

I could hardly tear myself away from the horses, and when I saw a groom at work on a beautiful black hunter it was all I could do not to seize a stable rubber and join in. I felt I would gladly have run about with buckets from morning to night in a place like that.

I asked Harry what he was going to be in the end, and he said of course he was going to be a famous rider and go all over the country competing in shows, and have a partnership in a good stable.

Meanwhile the Captain and Mrs Darcy had gone into the house, and as they came out I could hear shrieks and yells and out rushed the three Cholly-Sawcutt girls, April, May, and June.

I had had some experience – as I have told in a previous book – in teaching these three to ride, but like their father I had come to the conclusion that it was a hopeless task. It seems almost unbelievable that the

daughters of the great Captain Cholly-Sawcutt should
have been born incurably ham-handed, bouncing, and
completely without a sense of balance. But such was
the case. And like other people with such hideous
natural drawbacks they didn't realise how awful they
were – at least, if they did they didn't let it worry
them – but jogged happily about on their ponies and
entered for lots of competitions, and were excited
if they finished up anywhere but last. Their father
used to cover his face with his hands when they were
jumping, not in fear lest they might be thrown but
in horror because they looked so awful.

You couldn't teach them. Nobody on earth could
teach them. They were the Local Joke.

'Have you seen the foal, Jill?' yelled April.

'Isn't he a pet?' shouted May.

'We're going to the fête on Saturday,' shrieked
June. 'We've entered for everything.'

Their father gave a sort of hollow groan, and Mrs
Darcy said, 'Well, I've no doubt you'll all enjoy
yourselves.'

'Daddy said I was improving,' said April. 'You did
say so, didn't you, Daddy?'

'Did I?' said the Captain. 'I must have been mad.'

I thought, wasn't Fate funny to put three girls like
that into a home like that, when they would have been
so happy with somebody like Mrs Derry, going out
to tea and doing the flowers and learning tennis.

'Do come and see our ponies,' said May. 'That is,
if you're not in a hurry.'

Of course I am the sort of person who would go
with anybody to see anybody's ponies, but I wanted
to be tactful so I looked at Mrs Darcy first, and

she nodded as much as to say it was all right for me to go.

You will probably think I am going to tell you that the Cholly-Sawcutt girls had blood ponies of overpowering beauty, but such was not the case. Their father wisely realised that anything good would be wasted on them, so they had pleasant but very ordinary ponies of a strong and untemperamental kind, suited to their bouncy natures. And if you think these ponies were called by imaginative and romantic names you will also be disappointed because April, May, and June were not like that. The ponies were called by the dim and mere names of Tom, Bess, and Lad. They were kept in a small paddock of their own, but they had a nice little stable of their own too, and they each had their own stall and manger. Over each stall was a little wooden plaque with a letter painted on it in white paint, T, B, and L, and on three pegs hung three dark blue rugs, each having a white-embroidered letter, T, B, and L. I thought this was rather nice.

We gave the ponies sugar, actually far too much sugar as they were quite fat enough already, and June said, 'We've been doing quite a lot of schooling for the gymkhana on Saturday, much more than usual. I shouldn't be surprised if we won something.'

May said, 'I should! We never have yet.'

April said, 'It's awful having a famous rider for your father because the judges daren't give you a prize or people would think they were sucking up to Daddy.'

I was so taken aback by this absolutely preposterous idea that I could only open my mouth and stare at the frightful April. When I became conscious again I simply had to say, 'If you won a competition they'd have to give you the prize. Don't be silly.'

April said, 'Well, we never do win anything, so shucks to you.'

'We never win anything because we're rotten,' said June cheerfully.

I rather liked June. I said, 'Well, why don't you do something about it?' Only I really hadn't much hope for these poor girls, because of having been born the wrong shape for riders.

'It's too much bother doing anything about it,' said May, 'so we just go on being awful.'

And, believe me, this was true, they were content just to go on being awful, and if you are riders you will shudder at the thought just as I did.

Then June asked me to sign her autograph book, which she kept conveniently handy in a small corn bin, and she had got Ringo Starr in it and other world-shakingly famous people, in fact I wrote my name on the same page as Ringo Starr and it made me feel terrific.

I felt I had had the most wonderful afternoon and I hardly spoke all the way home.

Mrs Darcy said, 'I thought you'd be impressed, but you'd better come back to earth.'

16 The big day at last

It was a wet morning on the day of the fête, but everybody went round saying things like 'Rain before seven, fine before eleven', and funnily enough this turned out to be true.

I was busy all the morning, grooming the ponies and washing tails and hoofs. Then I packed all the grooming kit and the ponies' 'rewards' in the shape of oats and sugar. I don't know why I was so conceited as to think they would need a lot of rewards.

Then I ironed over my best shirt and tie, and brushed my clothes for the umpteenth time, and polished my boots, and as usual I couldn't find my riding hat and Mrs Crosby said, 'It's just the same old story about that hat of yours. If I were you I'd sleep with it tied round my neck,' and I said, 'I left it in the hall on its peg and I bet it was you who moved it,' and she said she wouldn't touch the silly thing with the tongs, not if it was ever so, and I said the whole point was to find it instead of arguing.

'It's all the same on these gymkhana mornings,' she grumbled. 'You just lose your head.'

'You mean my hat,' I said, not very cleverly.

I finally found it myself under a mac in the harness room and remembered that I had thrown it down there the day before, and Mrs Crosby

– who was a good sort in spite of being so fond
of a wrangle – brushed it for me and did it over
with some mysterious witch-like concoction which
she said 'brought up the black'.

I spent a long time dressing. We were all going
to travel in state in the Lowes' car, and Martin
Lowe had arrange to have my ponies taken over to
Blossom Hall.

The phone rang several times during the morning.
Everybody seemed to be going to the fête, and
everybody said exactly the same thing, 'Isn't it an
awful morning? But they say rain before seven fine
before eleven,' and I said, 'I jolly well hope so.'

At five minutes to eleven there was a bit of blue
in the sky, and at five past the sun was shining with
that steady look which means it intends to keep on.

Mrs Darcy rang up to say that she was setting off
at twelve thirty and would see me at the fête, and that
Sandy Two looked lovely and was in great form. I
dithered a bit at this. It meant that whatever happened
in the Novice Hack class it wouldn't be Sandy Two's
fault. I was thinking far more of Sandy Two than I
was of my own pony class.

I was dressed too soon and couldn't keep still, and
at twelve our cold lunch was on the table and Mummy
had stopped wondering what to put on and had gone
all summery in her cream silk.

When the Lowes drove up, Mrs Lowe said, 'All
roads today seem to be leading to Blossom Hall.
Everybody in the neighbourhood must be going.
It nearly seems to be rivalling Chatton Show as an
attraction.'

Martin gave me an encouraging smile and said,

'You look jolly good, Jill. I think you're going to have quite a day.'

I said that I had already been told that the judges were tough, and he said consolingly that the toughest ones were usually the fairest, which was something.

We set off, and it was an exciting journey as we kept passing horse boxes and parties of riders, all making for Blossom Hall, and I kept recognising people and waving.

When we turned into the gates of the park I saw that it had been completely transformed. There were marquees and little signposts and Scouts directing the traffic, and crowds of people everywhere. There was a turnstile with a long queue waiting to pay for admission, which was encouraging. Although the fête had hardly begun, the refreshment marquee looked to be full of people eating, and I thought how funny it was that when you are enjoying yourself it makes you hungry.

Mr Lowe parked the car, and their man was waiting at the car park with Martin's wheel-chair. We thought we had better go and see how the ponies were after the journey.

Just then I saw Ann calmly riding across the turf and yelled, 'Ann! Over here!'

She came over to us and said, 'So you're here. Golly, everybody's here! I should think Chatton'll be the original deserted village. I've seen Susan Pyke on her new half-Arab mare, and I nearly turned back because I don't think anybody else will stand a chance, except that she'll probably finish up with her arms round its neck and the judge having fourteen fits all over her. And Val and Jackie have each brought two ponies and they've got new black coats. I mean Val and Jackie, not the ponies. And James Bush is riding his father's Gay Prince in the open jumping and it's the biggest thing he's ever been in for, and his knees won't stop wobbling. Oh, and you'd scream! I've seen the Ghoul and the Zombie.'

These were two of our teachers from school and I said, 'Oh, yes, they've got a cottage near here,' and Mummy said, 'You really are the limit, why can't you say Miss Brace and Miss Peters?' and I said, 'Did you call teachers Miss Brace and Miss Peters when you were at school?' and she had to admit that her teachers had had other names too.

By now we were getting over towards the ponies, under the big trees at the side of the park. They all looked beautiful and their owners were busy putting the final touches. All our friends were there.

Black Boy and Rapide looked knowing and happy which always gave me confidence before a gymkhana. While I was fussing over their girths and bridles, Mrs Whirtley appeared, all in rose pink with an outsize pink hat. She was shaking hands with everybody all along the line of ponies, and saying how marvellous everybody looked and what a marvellous day it was, and when she got to Ann and me she handed us both a white satin rosette with a white streamer with Committee printed on it in gold letters, to pin on our lapels.

Ann said it was the first time either of us had ever been an official at a pony show, and Martin said, 'Who knows? You may be a judge some day,' and Ann said that as most judges appeared to be about eighty years old she wasn't very keen.

Just then two of the Committee boys came by pushing a yellow ice cream cart – which was their spell of duty – and they more or less blackmailed us into buying from them, so we each had an ice, and George got most of Ann's, which I thought was a bit rash as I wouldn't normally give ponies ice cream before a competition. But Ann said that if George was at all frustrated he didn't do his best, and if he wanted ice cream he just had to have it.

Mrs Whirtley said she had put in an extra showing class for the under-tens, as there was such a demand for it by infatuated parents who liked to see their infants looking so sweet on their ponies, and that was just about to take place, so meanwhile would Ann and I sell some raffle tickets for a superb iced cake?

We said we would, and it gave us a chance to wander round and see what everybody was doing. We sold a lot of tickets, though some people said they would have liked to see the superb iced cake before spending fifty pence, and why weren't we carrying it round with us? I said, 'Gosh, it weighs about a ton!' and Ann said, 'How much of the superb icing do you think there would be left on the superb iced cake if we carted it round with us in this heat?' Which seemed to satisfy them, and they paid their fifty pences, in fact a lot of people took one pound's worth, and we got over thirty pounds. Actually, we hadn't seen the cake, but if Mrs Whirtley said it was superb then it was, and in the end it was won by an old woman called Mrs Mains who was nearly ninety and lived in a one-room cottage in Billet Lane and hadn't any teeth, and some people thought she was a witch.

Mrs Whirtley brought the cake out of the house

on a lordly dish and everybody gasped and said Ooooh! and Mrs Mains said 'Lawks-a-mussy', and Mr Cuppleheaver the carrier offered to take it to the cottage for her on his lorry, and I'm quite sure that when the cake got into the cottage there wouldn't be any room for Mrs Mains. I often wondered what she did with it.

It is funny how people always win the wrong things in raffles.

Meanwhile the children's showing class was going on, and you couldn't get near the rails for the proud parents. There were some people who were only five, on Shetlands, and some frightfully efficient cool and collected ones of nine or ten. Ann said she would hate to be the judge. We both picked out the ones we thought would be placed first, second, and third, and we must have been pretty good judges because we proved to be right in two out of the three places, and it all ended up as baby classes often do end up, with some people in tears and others falling off their ponies with excitement at having won prizes.

The next was the under-fourteen Egg and Spoon, but though I had entered I didn't compete, as Mrs Darcy got hold of me and suggested that I should exercise Sandy Two. She tied on my number for me, and said, 'The ground is just right. Sandy is putting his feet down well, he likes it.'

I mounted and at once felt at home. Mrs Darcy came with me across the park to where several other competitors were exercising too. There were some lovely hacks, and one young man on a lean chestnut looked too incredibly good for words.

I walked, trotted, and then cantered Sandy Two

on a loose rein. I said to Mrs Darcy, 'Everybody else looks terribly good.'

'Now don't be silly,' she said in her forthright way. 'You're on the top of your form and so is Sandy. The novice test is quite easy and you know your stuff. I'm not asking you to win, I'm only asking you to do your best, and you're quite capable of perfection. You wouldn't want to compete against a lot of slugs!'

'He's a bit fresh,' I said, collecting Sandy Two who was trying to side-step.

'Of course he's fresh. The judges expect him to be.' Mrs Darcy added, 'You get down now, and I'll walk him about. This Egg-and-Spoon thing seems to be going on for ever.'

I began to wander across the park, and soon I noticed a large marquee, and full of curiosity peeped inside.

'Oh, hello,' said a voice, and there was my cousin Cecilia. It was her marquee. She was standing behind a long table covered with the most dismal articles of which she looked disgustingly proud. These were the handicrafts and Cecilia had made a lot of them herself and was waiting for them to be judged. There were a lot of knitted things, and some teacups with fat red roses painted on them, and some hideous brooches made out of acorns, and a lot of stuffed toys. There was a giraffe with staring eyes and a tiger made out of somebody's old pullover, and some chickens made out of grey blanket with combs of red flannel, and there were dozens of knitted woolly lambs. There was a very rickety stool with Bide-a-Wee painted on it in an awful shade of pink, and a purple satin cushion all frills, and some hard-looking bedroom slippers, and of course tons of Cecilia's own embroidery.

'Gosh!' I said. 'Do you have to stop in here all the time?' and Cecilia said she'd much rather, she was loving it. She said, 'Your coat collar's up at the back and you've got too much lipstick on.' I said, 'I haven't got any lipstick on at all,' and she said, 'Goodness! Do you mean to say your lips are that awful colour naturally? You'll terrify the judges.'

I said, 'I've just been exercising Sandy Two and I'm hot,' and she said, 'I thought good riders always stayed cool, I've heard you say so yourself.'

You just couldn't argue with Cecilia.

She said, 'If you can tear your mind from horses, come and look at the decorated dinner tables.'

What she meant was, come and look at the dinner table she had decorated herself. She led me past a lot of sweet peas and roses to her table. She had done it all in yellow flowers and it looked terribly impressive, though I couldn't help wondering what the food would look like with all that yellow round it. If you had been sitting at the table eating your dinner you wouldn't have been able to see anybody else who was sitting at the same table for all those flowers, but I suppose that doesn't matter in a competition.

I said, there didn't look to be much room for the stew and the vegetables and all the plates, and Cecilia said witheringly, 'Don't be silly.'

There were quite a lot of people in the tent, and you could hear what they said, and they all seemed to be admiring Cecilia's table very much. Of course the tables were numbered, and nobody knew who had done them.

Just then Ann came in, and said, 'Oh, there you are. Diana Bush won the Egg-and-Spoon and Jackie Heath was second, and I had the most awful luck, I lost my egg in the first heat. It's our showing class next, but there's heaps of time while they get the ring ready.'

Cecilia said, 'Oh, is that Ann? You look a bit of a wreck too.'

Ann said, 'Are you stopping in here all the time? Aren't you riding?' and Cecilia said she hadn't had any practice since she left Chatton, so she had decided to concentrate on the handicrafts, etc., and weren't they gorgeous? Ann said, absolutely terrific, but if any nervous kid saw that giraffe it would probably have a fit.

Then we both said good luck, we had better be getting along to the ring.

Black Boy was ready for the fray, and very nice he looked. There was an enormous entry for the under-sixteen showing class, and we looked like the Canterbury Pilgrims when the collecting steward called us into the ring. Half the people there I had never seen before.

I found myself riding behind Clarissa Dandleby, on a dashing blood pony. She sat too far forward and held it on a tight rein and was bright scarlet in the face. Behind me was Ann, on George, and I caught sight of Diana Bush on a new chestnut pony that was a bit too much for her.

We walked on quietly, except for the few people who didn't seem to know what a collected walk was, then we trotted and followed up with a canter.

At this point I saw Clarissa Dandleby in front of

me use her stick, and give her pony a whack that you could hear across the field. He bucked and then cantered on the wrong leg. The judge said, 'Number 31, stop using a stick,' and I thought, well that's the end of Clarissa.

Black Boy was going very nicely with his neck arched. Though he looked lively he felt very controlled and to my delight we were called in third. I didn't know the people in first and second place, but Ann was fourth.

Then the fun began. The boy who was placed first was riding a lovely grey pony of eye-catching showiness, long stride, and impressive action, and nobody was surprised he had been given first place, but when it came to reining back this pony proved impossible and would not stand in line. The judges waited for him for what seemed ages, and at last when he backed violently into the girl who was quietly sitting in second place a judge came over and said, 'Line up and stand, please.' At that moment he had to skip for his life, and his patience being exhausted he then told the girl and me to move up one, and sent the boy into third place. I was so pleased at being second that I didn't notice what happened next, because the girl was now doing her show. She did a very correct one, though I thought she was rather slow and and apt to swing off her balance, but it is a foolish thing in a competition to let yourself think another person is not doing too well, so I concentrated on keeping Black Boy standing squarely until it was my own turn.

My show seemed to go off quite well, and I looked round, to see that the boy who had been first had now given up even trying to control his too-fresh pony and was prancing off the field, and Ann was in third place.

The unsaddling and leading out went off without incident, and then the judges went into a huddle. They took ages deciding, but eventually left things alone and came up with the rosettes. I was very excited to get second, it was much more than I had hoped for, and I was so glad that Ann was third, in fact I wouldn't have been surprised if our positions were reversed. We cantered gaily round the ring with our rosettes, and when we got outside I remembered Susan Pyke and the half-Arab and wondered why she wasn't placed, but apparently she had found the pony too much for her, had crowded everybody else, and finally ridden right out of the ring.

17   Riding at the fête

The next class was Musical Chairs and I had entered Rapide, but I decided to scratch from it as I wanted to be fresh for the Novice Hack class which followed.

Ann said, 'Well, don't stand there for the next half-hour mooning over Sandy Two and getting the needle,' and I said I had no intention of mooning and would enjoy standing at the rails and watching the fun. I went and joined Mummy and the others, and Martin said, 'You did very well in that showing class, but I think you had a lot of luck. I never saw so many nappy ponies in my life. It beats me why people enter for showing classes when they can't even ride.' I said, 'I'm glad you weren't the judge or you'd have probably said that I couldn't even ride,' and he said that what I wanted to aim at was more elegance, and I said, 'Help!'

I was quite glad I hadn't entered for the Musical Chairs because it was murder. There were so many people in it that they had to do it in three goes, and even then the ponies were nearly in a stampede and people emerged from the scrimmage weeping.

All the parents round the ring were yelling and encouraging their own frightful offspring, and even ponies who knew their stuff from A to Z gave up trying and backed out of the mêlée to crop grass.

There was a thwacking of sticks, and the judges got furious and sent people out of the ring. Small red-faced kids kept crawling up to their mummies and saying it wasn't fair, the big ones had pushed them off the stools. Honestly, you couldn't hear the band half the time.

Eventually the whole thing was won by Clarissa Dandleby. She *would* win! She looked to me the sort of person who would win any war single-handed, being a born shover. I heard afterwards that she bit the boy who was left in with her at the end, and everybody was yelling so they never heard him shriek with pain and let go of the stool, and there was Clarissa sitting on it without a plait out of place and her glasses still on.

Martin said, 'Anybody who won that ought to go into the SAS. Who is she, anyway?'

I said, 'She's called Clarissa Dandleby and she's on the Committee and she hunts five times a week all through the season, and she's going to be a steeplechaser some day.'

Mummy said, 'She looks it,' and Mrs Lowe said, 'Well, she's not what I call a ladylike rider,' which was so understating the case that we all burst out laughing.

However, Clarissa was so thrilled to have won that you could see her gooseberry eyes popping right across the ring, and when she galloped round with her red rosette in her teeth her pony was covered with foam and we all felt very sorry for it.

Thank goodness I had kept calm and collected, because the next class was the Novice Hacks. Mummy held up her mirror for me to see that I was quite neat and then I went in search of Mrs Darcy who said coolly, 'Oh, there you are. Well, you look all right, but weren't you going to ride in your black coat?'

I gave one yell. Think of forgetting to change my coat! I absolutely flew to the Lowes' horse box where I had parked my things, and changed, and flew back again.

There was Sandy Two with his tail brushed out and his plaiting beautifully done. Even then I nearly went off without my number and Mrs Darcy had to tie it on for me.

'Will Class 4, the Novice Hack class, please come to the collecting ring?' said the loudspeaker.

As soon as I was actually up and riding I felt all right, though a bit dreamlike. Sandy Two was very fit and walked with a long, free stride. As we went round the ring I had a good look at the other competitors, and felt almost sorry that the competition wasn't very strong. Some of the other horses were bucking and some jogging instead of walking. There was only one outstanding one, and that was more of a hunter than a hack, ridden very competently by a farmer's daughter called Jean Nelson who always won a lot of prizes each season. I guessed Jean would probably be first.

However, I had to admit that Sandy was on top of his form and wasn't putting a foot wrong. He felt even more light in hand than usual, and went into his trot and canter with the utmost smoothness.

Jean Nelson was called in first and I was second. My rein back was good and Sandy Two stood squarely, so I resisted the fatal impulse to look down at his feet.

Jean Nelson's show was, I thought, perfect, but

mine seemed all right too. Actually I wasn't doing a thing, Sandy Two did it all himself. He took his inspection with a look of 'Find anything wrong with me if you can', and was perfect to lead in hand.

Then we waited while the judges made their minds up, though I couldn't think there was anything to ponder about. To my amazement when they finally approached I got the red rosette because they had decided that Jean Nelson's horse was more of a hunter than a hack and had given me the benefit of the doubt.

I rode out still feeling dazed, and Mrs Darcy met me and said, 'Thanks very much.' This was terrific praise from her, but I didn't deserve any as she had provided me with a perfect horse. I patted Sandy Two for ages and gave him sugar, and I felt very thrilled.

The next class was the Juvenile Jumping and there was a huge entry. A lot of people were in it just for fun, including April Cholly-Sawcutt who said she had been practising and could get over anything. Actually she was putting away ice creams up to the very last minute, and when her number was called she said, 'Golly! I forgot to show Tom round the jumps!'

We all watched Tom go over the bush jump in fine style, except that you could see the whole of the county through April's legs and she bumped down into the saddle with a thud that made Tom quiver all over, but he was strong and used to April. I guessed her father was groaning if he was watching. Then the crowd roared. Tom turned calmly round and took a bite out of the succulent top of the bush. April pulled him round and went for the wall at a mad gallop. Tom had by now decided that everybody concerned was out to play the fool, so he stopped dead, April shot over his head and landed on the turf with a resounding wallop. She grinned and got up, but Tom was by now halfway out of the ring, tossing his head about and trailing the reins. So that was the end of April's career, and we got down to the real business.

There were six jumps and none of them was very easy. Rapide had inspected them without showing any concern, but when it came to the point he didn't jump well. It just wasn't his day. He took the wall in a positive shower of bricks, and though he let me collect him he brought down the triple. I was very annoyed with him, but one doesn't show it in the ring, and he got his pat just the same as we left the ring. These things will happen.

I had plenty of time to watch the other people. Ann only got four faults, and up to then there hadn't been a clear round, but after that there were six clear rounds done by Val Heath, Susan Pyke (on the half-Arab, who certainly was a jumper), Clarissa Dandleby, and three unknowns. Clarissa went out at the first jump-off, and in the end Val was first, an unknown boy second, and Susan Pyke third. The standard had been high and the competition very keen, but when I congratulated Susan afterwards she wasn't at all pleased and said her father would consider it very *infra dig.* to be third on a pony that cost nearly three thousand pounds.

I said, 'What on earth has the cost of the pony to do with it? It's the riding,' and Susan said her father didn't look at it like that, so I began to feel sorry for Susan for having that sort of father.

Susan said in a nettled sort of way, 'Val's pony can't have cost a penny more than twelve hundred pounds,' and I said, 'Val is a jolly good jumper, she'd get the best out of any pony,' and walked off before Susan could annoy me any more.

It was now teatime and we had a wonderful party, sitting on the grass. There were loads of sandwiches and luscious iced cakes, and we topped it off with an ice cream or two and I don't know how many cups of tea. Our riding responsibilities were now over, and there was the open jumping to look forward to as well as Captain Cholly-Sawcutt's exhibition.

Meanwhile Mummy said she would like to see Cecilia's marquee so I took her over, and immediately we saw Cecilia in the middle of an admiring circle, being photographed by the local press. Her mother and father were there, and quite a lot of people who seemed to be her nearest and dearest.

She was standing by the stall and holding up a large piece of pink embroidery with a red card pinned to it saying First Prize.

'Isn't it nice?' said my Aunt Primrose, spotting us. 'Cecilia has won the first prize for handicrafts, isn't it marvellous?'

Honestly, the fuss that was made you would think Cecilia had won the open jumping at Wembley. Meanwhile the judges were making up their minds about the floral dinner tables, and while everybody in Cecilia's circle was still nattering on about her sordid embroidery, I was the one who came up and told her that her yellow flower arrangement had been placed second. So she had to go over and be photographed in front of that, holding up the blue card, and I thought Aunt Primrose was going to burst into flames with maternal pride. She kept saying she always knew Cecilia had it in her to do Great Things.

(When it came to giving the prizes later on it was an absolute scream, because being a charity affair they turned out to be articles not money prizes, and Mrs Whirtley had chosen nothing but horsy things for horsy people, so Cecilia got a riding stick for her embroidery and a hoof-pick for her dinner table, but Aunt Primrose said it didn't matter, they would come in for Christmas presents for somebody.)

By the time we got back to the ring there were thousands round it waiting to see Captain Cholly-Sawcutt's exhibition. In the middle of the ring was the local Silver Band, playing away like mad. We didn't get a very good view, but we could just see him when he rode in on Petronelle and the crowd went mad and gave him the most magnificent applause. The band melted way, panting a bit under their instruments, and there was the beautiful mare and the supreme rider alone in the vast green ring in the dazzling sunlight.

The Captain rode right round once so that everybody could see him. Then he dismounted and led Petronelle round the jumps. The ones we had used in the under-sixteen's had been taken away and the difficult ones erected in their places, and all we younger ones were dreaming of the day when we too should unflinchingly face jumps like these in open competitions.

Then the Captain came in for his exhibition round,

which was of course effortless and full of grace, and you never saw such beautiful timing. He went round the seven jumps twice, and at the fourteenth jump which was the triple bar he got a refusal and then brought the top bar down and got four more faults.

You should have heard the crowd yell. The Captain rode off laughing and making despairing faces.

Ann said she felt comforted to think that even the Great Could Fail, and Mummy said perhaps he had done it on purpose, and I said, 'Not likely. It's just one of those things.'

Near us Mrs Cholly-Sawcutt was standing with the three girls, and we heard May say, 'Hurrah, Daddy's made a mucker of it.'

April said, 'We'll never let him hear the last of this,' and June said, 'He hasn't got anything on us now, he's as bad as we are.'

Meanwhile, all the competitors had come in to inspect the jumps, and it was fun recognising the people we knew and admiring all the famous riders. You must have seen hundreds of open jumping competitions, so I need not describe this one. It was marvellous to watch, and there was always the excitement of not knowing quite what was going to happen when people who were expected to do well did badly, and people you didn't think were so good cleared four-foot-six jumps with inches to spare.

Six people got clear rounds, and among them were Mrs Darcy on Blue Smoke and James Bush on a new jumper of his father's, a long-backed grey hunter who had a wonderful sense of takeoff.

When it came to the jump-off we could hardly

watch for excitement. Two well-known riders went
out, and Mrs Darcy and James both got clear rounds
again and were in the last four. Finally Mrs Darcy was
second and James got the Reserve. Diana rushed off
to the paddock to congratulate her brilliant brother,
and we went too because we couldn't keep away from
the horses. Captain Cholly-Sawcutt was talking to
Mrs Darcy and admiring Blue Smoke, and we didn't
want to intrude so we were just oozing past when she
caught sight of us and the Captain called out, 'Hello,
Jill. You made a very good job of showing that hack.
I never saw neater work.'

I could feel myself going all the colours of the rain-
bow, and I mumbled something about Sandy Two
being so good that a child could have shown him.

Mrs Darcy said, 'Yes, I don't know anybody in
the junior classes who has a better knack of showing
than Jill.'

She so rarely praised anybody that I nearly fell flat
on my back, and Wendy Mead who had just come
up to lead Blue Smoke away and rub her down gave
me a grin and a wink.

'When do you leave school?' said the Captain to
me.

I looked a bit blank, as anybody would, at having
that sort of question fired at one in such a horsy
moment, and then I managed to mutter something
about 'it might be two years because of course I had to
get my GCSEs but I would be doing them next summer.'
I couldn't imagine why he wanted to know.

He just said calmly, 'Well, if you're wanting a job
after that I could use a person like you.'

I stood with all the breath knocked out of me,

trying to take this in. He gave a little wave of his hand, and said, 'Don't forget!' and walked off to join some friends who were waiting for him.

'Well!' said Mrs Darcy. 'That's a stunner for you, Jill. You're a very lucky girl.'

'D – did he mean it?' I stuttered, sagging at the knees.

'Of course he meant it. He's offering you a job when you leave school, and if you really want to make horsemanship your career it's the sort of chance you'll never get again. I'd have given my eyes for such a chance when I was your age, but nobody gave me one.'

'But how on earth would I ever get round Mummy?' I said.

She laughed and said, 'That's your worry, not mine. I've never known you to be very backward in devising ways of getting round anybody.' She looked round, and cried, 'Help! Everybody's getting ready for the winners' parade. Hurry up!'

I dashed off to get my ponies, feeling as if fireworks were going off all round me.

We all lined up and Mrs Whirtley came out to give the prizes. I got a pair of string gloves for showing Black Boy and a set of grooming tools for showing Sandy Two. They were just what I wanted, and I decided to hang them up in my tack room to give tone to the place, and go on using my old and rather scruffy ones. Mummy and Mrs Lowe came up to admire my prizes, and Mrs Lowe had saved some fruit cake as a special prize for Rapide and Black Boy, now that their day's work was over. I knew they didn't like fruit cake much, but they were too polite to spit it out so they swallowed it down and made faces at Mrs Lowe, and she said, 'Look, aren't they enjoying it?' and I thought, That's what you think.

Then who should appear but my cousin Cecilia, clutching her prizes, the riding stick and the hoof-pick, and she said that having won these very attractive things she was wondering whether to turn her attention to serious horsemanship, and what did I advise her to do? I said that if she was serious the best thing she could do would be to go to a good riding school and start from the beginning, and she said she thought it sounded awful, and I said, 'Well, it's that or nothing.' Personally I thought she would do better to stick to her own line of embroidery and decorating dinner tables, as she was so good at it. She seemed quite humbled and very kindly petted my ponies and said she thought they were marvellous, and I said I thought she had been pretty marvellous too in her handicrafts tent, and we became terribly friendly.

Then Mrs Whirtley got up on the platform, and the band sounded a sort of fanfare and hundreds of people gathered around.

Mrs Whirtley said that the day had been the wildest success, a far greater success than anybody had ever dreamed it could be. Everybody clapped and cheered. Mrs Whirtley said that her committee had worked terribly hard and been marvellous and everybody clapped and cheered again, except the committee, who blushed and looked smug in their white satin rosettes – that is, those who hadn't lost them. I had lost mine ages ago.

Mrs Whirtley said that of course they hadn't had time to count the money yet, but they were sure that it was going to be over three thousand pounds and it would all go to charities for the protection of horses. Everybody cheered like mad, and several people round me said, 'Gosh, three thousand pounds!'

Mrs Whirtley said that was the end of the proceedings, and now everybody could go home happy and contented, and just as she finished saying this there was a sort of disturbance on the edge of the crowd.

We all looked round to see what was happening. Everybody was looking the same way, and the crowd was beginning to give way and leave an open space. Mrs Whirtley and all the distinguished people on the platform looked a bit bothered. We couldn't imagine what was going to happen, but we soon knew.

The first thing I saw was a horse's head, and then my mouth came open and stayed that way. I nearly passed out. Into the open space walked three horses, and in the middle was a big percheron, and on its back was Dinah Dean, leading a pony on each side of her. She came calmly on amid the silent, staring crowd, who made way for her, wondering what on earth this was all in aid of. Dinah looked very determined. She came right on until she faced the platform. Then in a hush in which you could have heard a pin drop, she said in a very clear voice, 'If you really want to do something for the protection of horses, you can begin with these three!'

I have noticed in novels that when you come to a very dramatic bit, instead of putting Words Fail

Me, or some other phrase, the author just puts
row of dots.

So here they are.

. . . . . .

18 Dinah wins

'And you mean to say you knew all about it and kept it dark?' said Ann. 'You old Bluebeard!'

We were sitting in our orchard under the cool boughs, eating a peaceful apple or two.

'I knew she was in the woods with the horses,' I said, 'but I didn't know what she was going to spring on everybody today. It takes Dinah to think up something like that. She paralyses me, but she certainly does have ideas.'

Ann said, 'You could have knocked everybody for six when she rode up like that and started addressing the crowd. And gosh, what a speech she made! It was like a film.'

'And there we were in Mrs Whirtley's drawing-room when it was all over,' I went on, 'and Mrs Whirtley with her loving arms round Dinah, and Dinah putting away an enormous tea and being the heroine of the occasion, and answering the reporters' questions as cool as an ice cream soda! She's a wow.'

'And to think that that Towtle beast nearly bought Seraphine!' said Ann, looking pale blue. 'It was only your presence of mind that saved her, Jill. You must have been psycho-what's-it.'

I said that I didn't know about being psycho, it

was Mr Towtle's hair that put me off, and Ann said that Seraphine was now awfully happy with William Arden, and that Pam had got friendly with William and went over to the Ardens' to see Seraphine sometimes, and that Mrs Derry was relenting and talking about buying Pam another pony if one could be found that was quiet and aged enough.

I said, 'Good show,' but my mind still kept turning over and over the remarkable events of the afternoon and the dramatic ending to Mrs Whirtley's fête, staged and carried out by the fearless Dinah. I was sure it would be talked about in Chatton for years. In spite of my trying to keep my part in it dark, Dinah had insisted on grabbing my arm and saying to everybody, 'I couldn't have done anything if Jill hadn't been my friend, the only one I had,' and Mummy had laughed and said, 'If you'd told me where the loaves were going to I'd have found some jam to go with them,' and Mrs Darcy said, 'We all know that Jill can get away with anything,' and thumped me on the back. (At that moment a press photographer came up to take a photograph of Blue Smoke, who had won second place in the open jumping, and next morning there we all were in the local paper, Blue Smoke and Mrs Darcy looking marvellous, and me with my tie under my ear being thumped on the back as if I'd swallowed a fly.)

Things moved rapidly during the next few days. Captain Cholly-Sawcutt said that the Beastly Towtle would be forced to clear out of the neighbourhood after all that publicity, and never show his face again, and that the R.S.P.C.A. would keep an eye on him and his practices in future.

Mrs Whirtley kept Dinah and the three horses at Blossom Hall, and got so fond of the four of them that she couldn't bear the idea of being parted from them. In the end, to make everything law-abiding and above-board, she paid the Towtle creature strictly what the three horses were worth and gave them a permanent home with her, and what was more she said the riding pony was to be Dinah's very own, and Dinah was to have riding lessons and the pony would be looked after for her. Everybody went on making a fuss of Dinah and talking about Dinah until Dinah began to wish that she was an oyster with a shell, and that they would shut up and stop Doing Her Good, because it was altogether too much for a person who had never been accustomed to Being Done Good To.

Dinah's mysterious father then appeared on the scene. He looked very pale and worried and was quite a nice person really, though a bit absent-minded and thoughtless. He had been so wrapped up in his work that he just hadn't bothered about Dinah and didn't realise that she was being neglected. He was so glad to get her back that he nearly wept, and he came round to our house and asked Mummy what he could do to make things nicer for Dinah in future.

Mummy and Mrs Whirtley went into a huddle about what Mr Dean could do for Dinah. It turned out that he wasn't really very poor at all, but just never thought about money.

The end of it was that Mr Dean got a housekeeper, and Dinah was to go to boarding school – which thrilled her very much – and Mummy and Mrs Whirtley made a list of all the clothes she would need, and went shopping and bought them, and Mr Dean paid for them without turning a hair.

Dinah came round to see me. She had on nice clothes and had got her hair cut and looked quite human, in fact very decent. She had been to the library and got out a lot of books called *The Girls of St Agatha's, The Fourth Form at St Faith's, The Secret of the School*, and similar ghastly titles.

She said, 'I simply love these, and now I'll know what to do when I get to school, and in the holidays I shall have my pony and my lessons, and would you mind frightfully if I do a frieze of ponies round my room, like yours? If you think I'm a copy-cat, say so.'

I said I didn't mind a bit, but if I were Dinah I wouldn't be too sure that boarding school was going to be exactly like it sounded in library books, and Dinah said she was sure it would be, so I left it at that. I could see Dinah turning out to be The Blot of St Bertha's if she wasn't careful.

So all that died down, and I would be back at school again myself next week. And there was the winter to come, the lovely autumn rides through the crisp lanes, and November mornings on which to follow the Hunt.

I said to Mummy, 'It's been the best summer holiday ever.'

'Yes, darling,' said Mummy absently. She was having a tussle with *Basil the Bird-Song Boy*, who had stuck in the fifth chapter. She then became conscious and added, 'I hope you're going to work hard next term.'

I said, 'I certainly am – ' and was going to add all

about wanting to leave school next July, but when it came to the point I daren't and thought I had better wait for a more suitable occasion when Basil had got himself going again and Mummy was in a really mellow mood.

I wandered out to the orchard and saddled up Rapide and went for a ride. I couldn't think of anything but a future of horsemanship, beginning with grooming the Cholly-Sawcutt horses in chilly dawns and finishing up in the show ring at Wembley. It seemed like a beautiful golden dream, but it could come true.

I cantered along the grass verges of summery lanes, and when we came to Neshbury Common I let Rapide gallop to his heart's content and felt the cool wind blowing through my hair. I felt so happy that I let out a few hunting cries, and the rabbits, thinking I was mad, scuttered away in all directions.

MORE GREAT BOOKS AVAILABLE FROM KNIGHT